What's in Store

What's in Store

Poems 2000–2007

Trevor Joyce

New Writers' Press & The Gig
Dublin & Toronto
2007

Some of these poems previously appeared in the chapbooks *Take Over* and *Undone, Say* (The Gig, 2003).

This book is co-published by

New Writers' Press
61 Clarence Mangan Rd.
S.C. Rd.
Dublin 8
Ireland
email: newwriterspress@googlemail.com

and

The Gig
109 Hounslow Ave.
North York, ON   M2N 2B1
Canada
ph: 416 221 6865
email: ndorward@ndorward.com

More information about the author may be found at the SoundEye website: www.soundeye.org/trevorjoyce/

In addition to the people mentioned in the notes, acknowledge-ments and dedications at the back of this book, we wish to thank Thomas and Marla Dorward, Tony Frazer, Mike Hansen, Larry Kart, Bill Kennedy, Karen Mac Cormack and Steve McCaffery, Jean Missud, Marjorie Perloff, Jonathan Skinner and Isabelle Pelissier, Mark Truscott, Keith Tuma, and friends in Chicago (Eirik Steinhoff, Peter and Michael O'Leary, Joshua Kotin, and the *Chicago Review* crew) for providing much-needed encouragement and assistance as this book came together over the past eight years.

Text edited and typeset by Nate Dorward.
Cover designed by Gnocchi Artyst (www.gnocchiartyst.com).
Printed and bound in Canada.

Cover from a photo by the author, taken at Richmond Hill, Cork, May 2007. Author photo by Jessica Jones.

Contents (in brief)

Sets of untitled poems appear between the sections listed below.
A more detailed table of contents may be found on p. 315.

•

What's in Store

The truth
I dreamed
I craved
sweet fruit.

At the heart
of the mountain
seams of silver
shine.

Eat up, drink up,
enjoy yourselves,
while yet our shining
world survives.

Like flowers
in the meadow
we grow
and we thrive.

Like a hazel
nut shelled
we know
we must leave.

A birch tree
bends on the hill.
For a plough, girls chop
a handle.

That moustache,
is it your first?
For caps, girls braid
fine tassels.

I wore tassels
then I lost,
I had a lover
now he's left.

Don't wear tassels, girls,
don't lose out,
I lost my lover,
you need not.

Like last year's
winter wheat my hair
scarcely sprouted
and was shorn.

Like green timber
my soft bones
scarcely sprouted
and were shorn.

My poor Tolya
why go down
so early
into earth?

Why leave
just when
the blackberries
grow ripe?

No one foresaw
black worms would feed
on your fine figure
stood like a birch so white.

No one foresaw
black-headed worms would feed
on your fine eyes
so blue.

My Tolya,
my poor soul,
why have you said
goodbye so soon?

Let the speckled
cuckoo call,
a green field
is all it needs.

A handsome
boy to play along
is all a young
girl needs.

The wood is far,
the wood is dark,
a good horse
earns his keep.

When in the wood
I fell twin birch,
sweet love,
I think of you.

My father
was foolish,
should have raised
apple trees
not me.

If he'd raised
apple trees
instead of me
in summer
he'd have blossoms,
in fall
he'd have fruit.

Have you been
expecting us?
Have you fresh
beer set for us?

Cousins make
their way to us,
have you checked
at the window yet?

I set down oats
behind the barn,
now comes
the scythe.

Ah, my cousins,
my dear friends,
now comes
goodbye.

At break of day
the nightingale,
I thought my mother
called me home.

In the white night
the cuckoo sounds,
I thought my father
called me in.

Green the sleigh,
and blue the harness,
good colours
for a white-faced horse.

Behind your back
I speak your faults
however you
protest.

In the dark wood
swifts don't fly.
What's a blue dove
doing there?

With no mother,
with no father,
for you, what lies
in store?

On the garden
path
my mother
gave me birth.

She gave me birth,
she whispered:
sad days for you
my daughter dear.

In the centre
of the wood
an elm branch
goes unnoticed.

In the street
among my friends
I alone
am left unnoticed.

To work
we go
when the red
sun rises,

Home
we come
when the red
sun sets.
                Ay! Ay!

The golden
oriole rejoices
when the meadow
grass is shorn.

Our joy
lasts just
while we
are young.
                Ay! Ay!

Hey meadow
green meadow
bay horse
graze meadow.

I'll harness you
bay stallion,
I'll spancel you
bay stallion.

Don't harness me
good lad,
Don't spancel me
good lad.

I'm not a bay horse
I'm not a horse
I'm an outcast man
I'm a man cut loose.

One wing,
one wing,
a wing once cropped
is gone for good.

Cropped too
are we,
Allah assist us
to endure.

Hey! On a rock
high on the peak
I carved
my name.

Hey! When I climb
that peak my voice
rings loud,
I am alone.

The whitest of white
cloaks I wore,
then tried to mount
the whitest cloud.

That cloud bolted
and I missed
my chance to learn
the ways of God.

earlier
even than
morning

yet the
hands
are hard
at work

the maid
yawns in the
straightened
room

factotum
promenades

gun
cools
dust
settles

while the goods
are fenced

loan sharks
with lone
wolves
coevolve

world-up!

some treasure
hunters tired

their adept
dragoman
conjured
a city up
for their
refreshment

then he
disappeared
it

paf!

their quest
resumed

we
not notified
of this
arrangement
still tend bar
daily expecting
new customers

welcome!

not all
plants
are alike

some are
astringent
some are
salty

some sour
some sweet

some men
are short
-lived
some long

some ugly
others fortunate

weak strong
stupid clever
poor rich

was it
brevity
you wanted?

pot-bellied
thread-throttled
vomit-eaters
turd-lickers
void-pickers
vapour-swallowers
law-gobblers
water-slurpers
high-hopers
tip-topplers
spittle-hoovers
wig-eaters
blood-sippers
carnivores
smoke-sniffers
pus-dabblers
shit-twitchers
subterraneans
wonder-junkies
flare-burners
colour-fanciers
beach-bums
basket-cases
infant-eaters
cum-suckers
demoniacs
pyrophages
street-filth
wind-snackers
scald-tasters
toxin-takers
meadow-dwellers
ash-eating-tomb-trash
twig-perchers
street-corner-snorters
suicides

evidently
you are
confused
though one
cannot easily say
who with

even striking
beauty must go
camouflaged
some time

give us a clue

pierrot?
mr. president?
spy? terrorist?
the laughing
cavalier?

the whole thing
is intriguing!

beyond
neat roofs
ancient
irregular walls
protrude

grass
and taller
vegetation
thrives high

the escape
into deep
space
encompassed
is invisible
from the upstairs
window

sometimes
pigeons
scatter up

some day
the child
will go
look

Ritual

Should the goat consume the shed, women and children are convoked into the church, whilst the men fire shots with their rifles to dispel those great ants which, they fear, will in their turn devour the silly goat. This time is fraught with swallowing and dangerous. The priest rings the bells of his church, the children bang on saucepans with spoons. They make a silver storm. Events have each their proper hour. The goat must be afforded time to digest and fatten on the shed light. The breeze which riffles his beard is of that same tenuous plasma which blows the meat from our own bones. The children suck their forefingers and prod them in the air to determine the direction of flow. No idleness here! The din from the church in the middle of the night is dire and raucous. Before the church, menfolk valiantly discharge ancient shotguns in a cloud of rust. Within, the womenfolk draw down their ancient gods. Reverence and noise, terror, interpretation and awe: each to his own. And so it works.

Guidance

Training for ushers takes about a month and a half and includes instructions on greeting patrons, escorting people to their luminous treachery, collecting tickets and watching the country images.

"Anyone is allowed to become an usher. You don't have to be a student or even be involved in the war, although ushers of the age of 16 and 17 are about as young as we've had," he said.

And says that all an usher needs is a white shirt and black or navy pants or skirt. Cold hands are optional and cannot be taught. Amnesia and inefficiency may produce unexpected changes in a routine matinee idol so that repetition will be tolerable.

Ushering the throttled blue is not for everyone, although there are no requirements that voluntary ushers stay for the entire performance, many being unable to sustain the inconvenience, fury and intricacy. After a job is finished, ushers receive their credit and are free to go where weather will consume them.

Random Shifts

The hunt, with its frequent shifts and switches, its random* and idiosyncratic animal movements, its diverging multiple paths, opposes quantification, logic, stillness. Only through specifics is it worth. Consider that the best scent is that which is occasioned by the effluvia, or particles of scent, which are constantly perspiring from the desiderata as it flees, and are strongest and most favorable to the pursuant pack, when kept by the gravity of the air to the height of the breast; for then it neither is above their reach, nor is it necessary they should stoop for it. At such times, scent is said to lie *at the heart*, and is convenient. But this is only a slight part, for the chase comprises three distinct elements: the practical reason of the hunter, the instinct of the quarry, and the trap. We do not measure here our success in terms of truth, but in blood and experience.

* *Randonnée:* hunting term; the name of the course that hunters take in pursuit of their game

the change
is radical
and abrupt

difficult too
to account for

is it best
to trace
anterior
signs

originally
unrecognized?

this produces
a satisfying
continuity

an appearance
of reason

but the sheer
unexpectedness
is betrayed

normalized

time fears
the clock

burrows into
the folding
face-bones

conceals itself
inside the
voice

clock
comes with
diamond
minutes
sharp
with hours
and scissor
seconds

howl
honed
by cruel
corundum
days

leaves
speech
abraded
of affect

wiseguys
oddly disguised
refurbishing
a busted
flush with
sledgehammers
poached mesentery
follows
conspicuous
in candied
zest
despite
warnings
something condign
close impends
ladies
and gents
alterations
are most
pressing
exemplary
damages
which we
must next
account

hard words

no jawb
reakers though

nothing
obscure
in itself

no insults
either no
tonguelashing
or pieces
of anybody's
mind

instead
an oddly
constrained
formality

with fore
grounding
of occasional
details
specific
effects

surely it
must mean
something?

all that is the case

take first a crux take any crossing say take noon or
        ten to five
from it subtract the gravity the drag the I am not
        in pain

the year which passes and today and once before
the one who is about to get here just before the give to me
the house which we shall see exactly three days
afterwards the which the how the very book thou gavest

as while about to fall I saw thee while about to fall I saw
then the she who came here yesterday who will approach

tomorrow that that red box see it still is empty and so too
the green that tomorrow I will go away again and stay
with numeral intensifier and frequentative
the feverish am I intermittent fevers hold me tell

what now is left say can you play do you thirst
        very very much
in darkness the some days the street is sky and
        nothing else

now then

this room is empty   all
noise is the day everywhere
i haven't stopped remembering
being unsure   & the day is high
& warm outside   to say there is nothing
happening here would be
to exaggerate   it's
a slack one today said the sun
to the glass   let's us just say
that time encompasses the walls
here   (o flare of morning!)
that something is about
to happen   who are you?

speaking of what has happened

always some huge unseen
alters in the world
between each flicker and the next

consequent apprehension comes
not like an autopsy
whose subject should be dead

but through divisions
of the living breath
that is one whole

from first cry to the end
though it accelerates or slows
by turn grows clear

or close or dull or fine
mastering like a weather
the exposed attention

shivering after makes report
it rained was sunny for a while
then came a storm

a complete
world

trees
beasts
birds
and men

is realized
in whiteness

cool blue
white
of the pruning
peasant

cream of the
milking
herdsman

fleece
of a different
blank
again

the wind
is in the sky

the void

certain
virtuosos
dug chunks
out of it

shaped them
for tears
laughter
pity

others
automated all
for speed
and efficiency

drilled
sympathy
controlled
joy and terror
dwindled

yet vestiges
persisted
through habit
and politeness

cosm is
anxious

fidgeting

has all
the trappings
of the familiar

saving least
promise
of comfort

keeps flapping
like a bird
after long flight
unable to find
a place of rest

we have
been here
before

shadows
a crude
dramaturgy

aspires
to the condition
of philosophy

oracle
even

incongruous
bonus
to us

provides
mechanical
ponies

to facilitate
comprehension

how often

how many
times

can such
clichés
be recycled

we ask
ask ask

what happened
to novelty
originality

cost
which is
pitiless

travels
at its heels

like a starving
tiger that pursues
the labourer
through the fields

or some
wretched
mongrel
scavenging
these stone
estates

yes

exactly
like
that

suddenly growing
sentimentally
attached
to the poor
world

jabbed
pathetic
thorns into the
inanimate

then watched
roses rock
with laughter
conurbations
weep and gnash
vast systems
bleed
in sympathy

unfeigned
reciprocity
is a great
thing

no?

Saws

1

flame has a skin of cold
light sets limit to the dark
so name me then
the outside rind of memory
the clothes love wears

•

rock in the streambed
fluid thats your element is absence
complex with vortices and currents
bears cold against the bone
still hand reaches grips itself

•

silence vexed
touch when presence would suffice
anatomizing scrutiny
break the made whole
care gathers mute blind here

•

faulting crowd from fend
touch impairs the waist the small
the shoulder prompts the touch
as instruments diminish even to the heart
needs must intents persist

•

spontaneously sight unseen
in the intervals between
where venture hunts its gain
beasts may become familiar
and grow tame

2

hold friends and colours and sleep fast
inch an abyss ocean no barrier
truly the execution is woeful
passion suffers where the flimsy heart
wont break wont break

•

chance set of winds you
fixed deck of bones you
my chambered and mined
my furnished with tables
my table of cases of tides

•

the water touched
deteriorates and gains
last of whats passing
first of whats to come
robs and returns

•

action dons habit of effect
sleight uncontrolled
ghosted out from us
how ever to come to again
if we nothing have laid down

•

every sake acknowledged serves
this am traversed by words
provisional coherence
interim and out of sorts
able for joy

3

mirrors eclipses departures
loss instantaneous or slow
barren doubling
death is all we see awake
and sleeping only sleep

•

fronts and systems move across
through the weather of such data
drifting hungers and accessory rage
you claim with care your personal effects
as general consequence accrues

•

no cage is found for wind or rain
so older than desire that stirs the hand
prior to relief to grief to nerve and nerves
what by the heart
is hidden hidden is

•

structures unseen the seen decide
you near space intervenes
gone head will conjure head the lid the lip
waking we share and sleeping turn aside
eyes twinned make the world deep

•

have you forgotten
that past is anyhow indelible
scape from its map withdraws
to lodge at heart in dream through fright flight poised
map gone you have forgotten nothing

after
the fun
night
closes
down
the empty
rooms

she has
a figure
this one
and what
hair

but see
the posture
is unnatural

if it gazes
long
unblinking
at the
dark
then
it's not
real

travelling
unawares

has packed
all and too
much so
overequipped
for any
reasonably
foreseeable
situation

all familiars
at the ready

graceful phrase
smile compact glass

so encased
by apparatus
is she

what a shock
to arrive!

i grieve
for her
hair

gold
glistening

kindles
as she
tears it
out

nor can
her tears
ever be
dried

all this
displeases
me

worst
to see her
damage
that face

which has not
deserved it

excess
of seeing
turned
her eyes
to milk

whiter
than eggs

softer
than clouds

they dream
across
her face

venus
they say
had an arse
of straw

cold stars
wheeze
at the gable
end

don't
go

brilliant
hard
cold
colours
should be
avoided
by mature

so strong
are they
that they
deprive
the wearer
of all
natural
pigmentation
of skin
eyes
hair

robbing
even a
young
vigorous
girl
of animation
and charm

a very
ugly
effect
may result
from comb
ining two
different
tones
of the same
colour

so we
say
one
blue
kills
another

one
red
kills
another
red

simultaneous
contrast
triggers a
disastrous
result

exercise
great
care

i put on
this surface
to disguise
my deep
and shallow

you mistake
my limits
for myself

neglecting
my forests
my cliffs

sometimes
herds
of cattle
run to the edge
and plunge

later
silvery
cascades
descend

Sonnet

Drink hard, girls,
If you're smart.
Alcohol elevates,
Love lacerates
The heart.

Pearls
Don't grow on trees,
Curls
Catch devotees,

So fast,
Put your face on,
Be bright and brazen,
A doll doesn't last
If she can't seem to please.

Hoofing It

o my belle saboteuse of fur mukluks and pac boots,
o sweet stiletto, astragalus mine galoshed;
swish me in jodhpurs, chukka me, granny me thighways,
then your sesamoid swivel to this zygoma's bliss

Action Sequence

Great gals gone west
into millions of sunsets,
claiming *absence*
my presence is,
strangeness my grace,
as whackers and knackers,
sad slackers, court packers,
sundry vatic pragmatics
are with axes and tumbrils,
old agues and age,
all adroitly despatched,
amid armies of leggings
and earrings of ice, there
there is felt a nice
nostalgia for ambiguity.

One thing's for sure — the
sub-basement deportment
department's not there
for your bloody idle amusement.
Mother Teresa, Peggy Sue?
They're all deported, Helen too.
The dominant is melancholy,
and not by subs or doms
or four-letter bombs can I be
comforted. "Entertainment"
you call it? Yes, and "God
will provide." Sure! We'll all
sleep easy on the other side.

Combing

thimbles of plush
throng between us

buzzing their wingwork
their excreta sweet

Levels

A sharp skill of benches,
A soft volley of shots;
Imperfection of dies
Thrown goes unnoticed.

A sheer lack of tolerants
With shattering of glass;
A corporate culture
Of firm forward plans.

A vessel of fragments,
A shock of depression,
A nice can of worms,
A form of expression.

Manufacture of parts
That are moving.
A speaking of parts
That are moving.

An emergence of fresh
Growth in the spring;
Fall, parching of tools,
Dry instrumentality.

Dimension of quiet,
Dimension of lies.
An image of death.
An extravagant task.

how one
carries
oneself
matters

some easily
negotiate
the most
awkward
situations

the face
only very
occasionally
moist
distorted
or the throat
agape

entry
and exit
smooth
as if supported
by a race

of steel
spheres

image knows
simultaneously

both event

and the
precise
formal
arrangement

this is
poise

arriving
neither
too early
nor too
late

withholding
the sharp
observation

the untoward
move

so our host
can show
happy

manners
cost
nothing

this is
normal
i tell you

they'll
be friends
again when
they've
done

blaming one
another
for doubtful
wrongs

gesticulating
making
one another
bleed
for words
misunderstood

or one
wants
to go
and one
to stay

a baker's
dozen
comprises
each such
quarter

count
but hide
your hand

whether steel
blue serge
or simple grey
the art is
in the fit
the fitting in

why must there
always be a court
involved?

abashed
by her
voice
he crawled
forward
on his belly

tongue
lolling
eyes
idiotic
with craven
humility

she stooped
her touch
magic

propitiation
turned
ecstasy

he began
to yelp
and cavort

a shower
of chromatic
notes

this mis
fortunate
bitch

may never
walk again

something
with the nerves
they say

perhaps
the spine
suffered
some trauma

whimpering
occasionally

she sleeps
until they
come for her

again
the nose
flares

forelimbs
scrabbling
dreamt
earth

numbers
and cyclic
repetitions

we abstracted
from stars

exhausting
those high
habitats
of deities

regularity
conserved
in calendars

in clocks
constructed
out of
water
sand
or wheels

and so
can set
the exact
hour
for dinner

presence
of the angel
of death
is generally
acceptable

even following
a series
of happy
scenes

it adds
a certain
weight

difficult
to achieve
by other
means

having small
children
play naive
divinities
may also
work

this statue
commemorating
an historic
electrical storm
represented
carved in salt
on a plinth
of winds

itself now
stands
in terror
of rain

and you laugh
heartily
at its predicament

what way is that
to behave?

Spring Comes

past scope of silk
stirrup and bow
undergo refinement
as incoherence
regulates the sands

Scene vividly displays, in a mild transform
    of the received,
Flowering branches penetrate throughout the
    ancient yet intact.
Courts and corridors, row on row, are solemn,
    majestic and impressive,
Green tiles load the eaves, terraced pavilions
    cancel curious eyes.

Conserved together, one hundred and nine
    people appearing lifelike,
At different ages have distinguished
    identities, tics, composures;
Gestures and actions are varied, whether at
    flowers or holding things;
Laughter at birds' play by the verandah, then
    haste smart coach to the midyard.

Consorts are ensembling the bamboo flute,
    drum, pipe and chime stone;
Engrossed at chess some ponder, while others
    more at ease are dressing;
Some enjoy fish, tease parrots, paint long
    recessions of unbolted doors;
Harness and armour glint at the gate, generals
    bow, reign in their hearts.

Varied posture and colour of the imperial
  concubines
In bright peaceful and happy deluxe like
  we like;
Luminosity so intense night will
  plunder,
Awkward dark stranger, uncouth invader.
  Mercy!

Clustered peonies, towering pines, peacocks
  in glorious exhibition
And red-crowned crane shouting at
  each other;
Purple camel-humps seethe agreeably in
  viridian glaze;
All is blended, and implied meanings are
  deep, implicit and rather fascinating.

Composition is exquisite, layout clearly
  demarcated.
It gives a splendid scene of the gentle people
  echoing and mixing in.
The plot of false or true, moving or still, has
  been organically linked.
Truly monstrates natural interaction, is worth
  seeing a hundred times.

From the *Thesaurus Novus*
of Petrus de Palude

As Alexander approached
Eden, an old man was pursued
into a steep defile
by an advance party.

They at once detained him
as an enemy combatant,
but the greybeard signalled
weakly, and they stopped.

"Go tell Sir Alexander,"
said the man of years,
"that he seeks paradise in vain;
his striving is all futile,

for the highway
to paradise is a lowly
course, a course
he does not know.

Take you this stone,
give it to Alexander, saying,
'This stone sums
your worth.' "

Now the stone
was of inestimable value
and of excessive weight,
very paramount of gems,

but spun to dust
was as a wisp of hay,
and of less worth.
By which sign

the venerable
represented
Alexander living
king of kings,

Alexander zero dead.

Romance

Brisk as a goat my father is since he resigned
his instruments of war; the ambit of his rule reduced,
constrained, become eccentric, in wild epicycles now
the royal bones rotate that with his dislocated court process.

Skull still twirls attentively, bright eyes
spy back, mouth seizes fast on opportunity.
My mother goes beside him shallow as a pond.

Enchambered deep and happy as a trout
my own sweet lady circulates, scarcely at all
discomfited to find her gossips fresh
detongued, unsighted and her men unmanned,

since all devoted still to servicing her wants.
Something. There is something between us.
Yet she is quick which certainly must compensate

to her for those, her family to two degrees,
whose breath for the securing of our state
was earlier interrupted. Our close physicians expertly concoct
for her electuaries and nostrums of sure bliss.

How Oshun got sight

Time came a conclave
of male spirits excluded her.

She raged.
Made women barren.
Made ghosts afraid.

Gold and copper,
these were offered to her.
She turned away.

They offered her honey.
She turned back.

Time came a spirit
of scrying walked
into the water,
washed himself.

His clothes were stolen.
He wept, he raged.

Oshun heard him,
said, "I get your clothes,
you teach me sight."

Her skin she made
sweet with honey.
Yellow scarves
she tied at her waist.

She walked
to the spirit thief.
She was beautiful.
He gave the clothes.

She got sight.
She crossed
in the slave-ships.
Honey is offered.

Séan O'Duibhir a' Ghleanna

Through the early sunshine
of this summer morning
hounds raise up their howling
    while the sweet birds sing.
The small beasts and the badger
keep covert with the woodcock,
all lie low from the echo
    and the booming of the guns.
Fox red on rock keeps lookout
on the horsemen's hurly-burly
and the woman by the wayside
    lamenting scattered geese.
But now the woods are levelled
let us leave familiar landmarks
since, Séan, my friend, it's over,
    the game is up and gone.

That's why I sing of sorrow
bone frozen to the marrow
as the north wind comes to winnow
    and death is in the air.
My dog, my dear companion,
is leashed without the freedom
you'd give a child to cheer him
    in the bright noon of the day.
On crags, the royal stag bounding
bears his antlers proudly
and he'll run on through the furzelands
    till the last day of this life;
if I had no more harassment
from this town's petty gentry
I'd take ship out of Galway
    and leave off these wild ways.

The homesteads of Glen Srutha
lack loft or roof among them,
in Sráid na gCuach a silence
    substitutes for praise;
Harsh weather without shelter
from Cluain to Stuaic na gColm,
the hare beside the headland
    unharried all its days.
What is this human tumult
with so much fell destruction
the sweet thrush and the blackbird
    find no twig for song?
Sure omen of war's onset,
to see priests and people troubled,
driven to harsh havens
    among the upland glens.

My one regret this morning
that I did not die reproachless
that time before the scandal
    caused by my own kind,
when many the long bright evening
saw apples crowd the branches,
when leaves enclosed the oakwood
    and dew was on the grass.
But now I am an outcast,
lonely, far from friendship,
I lodge alone in thickets
    and fissures in the rock;
but unless there's no harassment
from this town's petty gentry
I'll leave all my possessions
    and so resign my soul.

Limitless

In the routine melancholy of its song,
note the exact bird roost;
though still its heart goes beating on
very functional and fast,

in the perfected structure it must hurt,
the flawed parasite, too, stop for good,
though the time be short,
though the time be short,

hidden by the general wood
predator strangely hesitate.
What memory, so smooth, supplants
grief and desire obliterate.

Listen: beyond the buzzing
of the light the inarticulate
bushmeat is howling,
the insensate pelt grows fearful too.

Is all that out of earshot?
Well, then, get this:
seeing their zenith slip
tongues lose their lexicon yet plead

with orchestration of the blood;
and always, through the heart, the hand,
the eye, the rib-bone or the spine,
that same immemorial wound.

The unfamiliar names sit neat
with practiced pain, but nebulous
beside the sharpness of the intimately known,
the precise experience;

troupial, finch and condor,
freed from a longing not their own,
fly up, not crippled, their sly strength
innocent, intending no transgression.

To Lily Bloom

O Dear, my twentyseven senses' dearest, theeward
     I love!
Thou'd one, of thee, theeward, thou done, then
     theeward I, thee meward — we?
Which, come to think of it, fits neither here nor there.

Who art thou, Madam unaddable? Thou art, art thou?
Wert once they say.
So let them say, that yet don't get it, how the
     steeple stands.

Thou goest forth with hat on foot, and art afoot by hand,
Handwise thou footest fleet.

Hello, hello, your red getup, faulted in white folds.
Red do I love Lily Bloom, red theeward I love!
Thou'd one, of thee, theeward, thou done, then
     theeward I, thee meward — we?
Which, come to think of it, goes as the fire goes, out.
Red Bloom, red Lily Bloom, what do they say?

   A bonus question:
   1) Lily Bloom has a cockatoo
   2) Lily Bloom is red
   3) What colour cockatoo has Lil?

Blue is the colour of your yellow hair.
Red is the cooing of your green cockatoo.
Plain girl got up for everyday,
You dear green beast, theeward I love!
Thou'd one, of thee, theeward, thou done, then
     theeward I, thee meward — we?
Which, come to think of it, goes with the ash to the
     dump my dear.

O Bloom, my Lil, O L — I — L,
Thy word drops out of me.
This word of thee runs soft as wax.
Have you got that Lil, have you got it clear?
One can also read your rear my dear,
And thou, thou most miraculousest,
Art afterward as foreward:
L — I — L
The tallow tears AFFLICT my rump.

Dear Lily Bloom,
Thou sleeping beast,
Theeward — I — love!

eye
masked
behind
its own
force

mouth issuing
fears and agitated
reminiscence
through which
both threats
and pleadings
are sensible

fists beating
feet pacing body
twisted between
vehement
extremities

ah yes

you are
trafficking
in feelings

matter
of age
illness
poverty

though generally
too depressing

are used
to demonstrate
knowledge
of the world

thus strengthening
the work

mention
of sport
dancing
recreational
drinking

handled
with the
effect of
spontaneity

has wide
appeal

truth is
i'm going through
a bad patch

this weather
isn't helping

grey days till we
had quite forgot
the sun

and always
those same
ponderous
swine gather
here to eat

i greet
and am
polite

i will
to work
the tradesman
said

observe
the elbow
greasing

though
marketable
men
be mice

and tradewinds
are decreasing

take oh
take
my breath
away

never
never
change

you are
my everything

be still
unceasing

what was
is not

she has
destroyed
many
pictures
much
correspondence

it is good
to take
an interest
in the imaginative
preparation
of food

now she
has made
new friends

continues
still to trust
brute
animals

as if
there were
morning
and yesterday

as if
sun
wasn't
moon
wasn't
stars

in the
faint
light
of remote
galaxies
you spin
and fall

faster
i
traverse
you
vengeful

dusty
zero
too
ineffectual
to fix

stone
human
sky

bedded
three-ply

colour
leaching
levels
down

air glows
diaphanous

sediments
obscure

as human
sentiment
grows
colourable
memory
is heavy
freight

sky
exalts
light

cold sumps
black out

the heart
is a chambered
habitat

let's have
a market
in affects

bulls
gravitate
to rage
bears to
disproportionate
sadness

shorts
considering
happiness
overvalued
are active
there

options
offer
profits
with
significant
risk

secondary
markets
trading
used
securities
are deep
and abject

it is not
unknown
for the eyes
to continue
blinking
intermittently

one equals
yes twice no
tears don't
count

then can
the mouth
still crave
still offer
pleasure?
nose
experience
disgust?

what pains
the phantom
heart?

She is my love
　　was most my misery
preferred for wasting me
　　to her could cure

She is my fair
　　would fast enfeeble me
not whisper for my going oh!
　　or mind my grave

She is my dear
　　nature's accessory
wouldn't reach a hand to hold my head
　　lay me for gold

She is my why
　　drops not a hint to me
heeds no true word
　　spares no regard

Great is my grief
　　too long this lingering
who most suspects me
　　is all my love

I will not die for you
O woman like a swan, withdrawn,
You've wrecked your share of fools,
Remember they weren't me.

On what account would you have me wasted?
For the red mouth, is it, or the flowers within?
For the seeming soft, or the swan-like breast?
Tell me, are those to die for?

Those upright breasts, that perfumed skin,
The blushing cheek, the ruffled nape?
Assure yourself I'll never die
For them, God be my help!

Fine your eyebrows, gold your mane,
Safe your secret, slow your speech,
Neat your ankle, smooth your thigh,
But I'm not the fool would die for them.

Sweet your pleasure, yours your choosing,
Slight your palm, like foam your flank,
Blue eye, white throat,
I will not die for you.

O woman like a swan, withdrawn,
I studied with a cunning man.
O slender hand, white throat,
I will not die for you.

I'm not gonna die
little lady
I'm not gonna die
for you
so get used to it

Cos why would I die
if I was gonna die
gimme a good reason
red mouth honey mouth
gimme a break why doncha

Sharp tits sweet skin
don't make the grade
any more little lady
or the blush or the ruff
-led nape no deal

So I'm not gonna sigh
little eyebrow pen
-cilled bottle blonde
for your fashion heel
and your well waxed thigh

Sure you pleasure well
and you know what's what
with your haunch foam
bright and your eye pure
blue but I'm not gonna die

for a milk white throat
or a slender hand — I studied
with a cunning man and I'm not
gonna die for you little lady
no I'm not gonna die today

is one
with a
fedora

trenchcoat
belted
at the waist

collar
up

and yellow
calfskin
gloves

a polished
shoe shows
below the
trouser-cuff

but know
the sole
is worn
through

and only
the appearance
is indestructible

a man
in civilian
clothes
approaches
a military
policeman

says
i am
a deserter

what
should
be
done?

he must
be given
over to a
constable
for a
rraignment
before a
magistrate

further
questions
will
inevitably
arise

if lighters
are used
pad gently
underneath
with straw
or matting

similarly
for a wharf

remember
horses
slung over
a ship's
side
by crane
are apt
to fall
on their
knees
when they
first
touch
ground

admit no
vendors

they sell
you eggs
and poultry
roaming
camp
all day

at night
they snipe
industriously
into you

let the
men
sleep
upon their
rifles

tribesmen
are wonderfully
cute
at stealing
rifles

detail
sentries

calamity
calls out
fidelity

mark that
with choice
medallions

trailing
rainbows
of silk

have winged
victories
enact vast
conquests
cast in dull
alloys

these be
affixed
above
the heart

pin can't
hold it?
try a nail

Neglect In Camera

It is another obscure chamber. The town is trapped in light and shade, and limited to the back wall of the shop. The glasses man and his parrot inhabit an intermediate dimension.

The parrot knows the names of things. *Roskyn,* he says. Then, *shag, cendal, gazzatum, dobby, fleece.* An ignorance of grammar does not allow his speech to accumulate meaning. His master draughts the projected image on his scrim. Things he knows, but not their names.

They make an odd pair, this glasses man and his pet. When the bird dies, his master will have him stuffed, he loves him so. Already selected is the corner in which he will perch, steadfast. The figures moving through the inverted silver town are averaged into a poised stasis. They represent the citizens as the bird represents the tropics.

Later, the glasses man will attend with oils to the precise textures of cloth, of hair, of milk pouring, a needle penetrating lace, sunlight on pearl, on skin. His nails are dark from years of grinding colours. His eyes are dark from years. His skin? *Gossamer!*

Lecture on Seven

From a medical and scientific standpoint the digit seven is a signal point of calculation. The entire system is wholly transformed every seven years: there are seven stages of prenatal existence, the brain takes seven forms before assuming its unique character, and so on. Throughout history the number seven has played a determining role: how many are the races of man, his wonders, planets, days, colours, minerals, senses; how manyfold is each of the three parts of the body, how ply the shooter's little natural, or the divisions of the world? Say, to which number does the Bible accord greatest importance? Say then no more.

Take that the entire system suffers heptadic change. These alternate sevens resemble the functional changes of the body. A child slight at seven is likely also to be so at twenty-one, whereas a hulking seven will again be hale at twenty-one, no matter how frail the intermediate years. It follows that every line on the hand can be divided into sections giving dates with more or less accuracy.

Paramount, however, and most usually consulted in reference to dates, are the life and fate. Observe how the line of fate comprises three great divisions at twenty-one, thirty-five, and forty-nine, and from this build the very life-grid. Note down the class or type of hand before proceeding or attempting the smallest. It stands to reason that there must be variation between hands of the different destinies. Bear this in mind, and skew in accordance with the life of the palm. Mentally to characterize and age the lines as shown you will find simplest and most accurate.

Use life and fate together, and they corroborate to specify the events. It is therefore not difficult, after a little practice, to tell when an illness or an event took place, or when such and such a thing will happen, be it a party, outrage or a death. Practice brings perfection in all things; let not the student be discouraged, therefore, if at first he finds difficulty in dividing the lives into divisions and subdivisions. Such things take time.

that drop
like a magnet
tugged at
everything
high

often i
would watch
it suck in
birds
aircraft
and towers

i closed
my eyes
whenever
i heard
mountains
creaking

even
happiness
imagination
and playfulness
fell in

as in
another
man
a clot
might
tour
quite
happily

until
it struck
his brain to
kingdom
come

in him
a rancour
appeared
to circulate

so that
at inopportune
moments
his head
would
start
pleading
angrily

right
shoulder
red?

from vein
of neither
bird
nor beast

that ship
lacked keel?

all tenders
demand care

calendric
thumb
and thimble
push

the flashing
past

they rear
and scamper
back

ragged bones
terror
so selved

nothing
accomplished
but return

yet for this
he is celebrated

for this
beasts
are roasted
provisions
squandered
inheritance
dispersed

the other
must not be
forgotten

he is unloved
neglected
and he is
capable
of great
hurt

speech?
stopped

sight?
blocked

face?
a total loss

slept always
in high
chambers

nightmares now
among deep
roots

left once
never returned

youth has
its amplitude

say who
lives longer
than the infant
dies at birth?

I have spent

entire months trembling
whole seconds being compassionate
several moments wondering
many nights alone
innumerable days unmemorably
too long forgetfully
hours together hours together
saying now is my time

Skinbone Sing

Went to the market
      there was red there before me
      wearin a tailored suit
Said, red, what you doin
      why you go crawlin
      sideways on the dirt?
Red just said nothin
      climbed back up on them bones
      kept on movin

Stood there
      grit in my shoes
      hurt my walkin
      couldnt tell
      west from east

Held a few favorites
      the rest lost or broken
When the day turned blind
      heard crashin through the dark

Wanted something else
      didn't have a name for
Wanted something else
Found a three-piece of ice
      thin-striped with flame
      and too big
Wanted something else
Didn't know there was made
      sheets of milk
      would have wrapped
them around me

At the wrecked gate
     red ran by like a target
     he was scared
     his tongue flickered
     he had on a suit of straw

Maybe somewhere
     under a rock

Kindling

i put wood in the fire
when no one was about
now there's fire in the wood
and i can't put it out

storm
across
the mind
dismays
this one

thought is
precipitate
is always
incompleted

fragments
disperse quite
unavailable
to memory

yet it must
somehow pull
itself together

name
birth
address
reasons

forms are
to be
filled out

streets vacated
quarters abandoned

what this
thing is?
what for
it is?

no knowing

the owner has
dumped it
with the scatter
of useless

isolation
at the awkward
corner

loneliness
in the cramped
room

exposed
faces

i dig
my ten
nails
into the
door

they are
like the
scribbling
of a child

like the
imprint
of a bird's
feet

like the
scars
of an old
wound

the efforts
of a starving
man

when
someone
is eaten
up with care

the standard
technique

the manner
of wielding
knife
fork
spoon
plate
serviette
and other
utensils

is not
employed

it is a most
uncivilized
business

let's turn
to something
else

the marvellous
bird
won't sing
on every
branch

i don't
always have
a quilted
bed

pity me
wait for me
turn to me
kiss me
pity me

red apple
eating
straw bale
sleeping

turn to me

In the small hours
        far too highstrung,
make the zither
        twang.

Gauze curtains catch
        the moon,
wind chills
        the skin.

Hear, in the far marsh,
        one wild goose call;
throngs swoop and sing
        up north in woods.

Pacing, pacing,
        sight itself shuts down;
misery shrinks
        the isolate heart.

Under orchard
     peach and plum
     stray trampled paths,
but when wind burns sere
     the leaf
     the fall sets in.

Bright flowers fade,
     the thorn
     walks in the hall.

So saddle up and ride
     into the everlasting
     high sierras.

Your own time short, what form
     should love
     of wife and children take
when all across the level lands the grass
     stands white,
     cold darkens in?

Blood-sweating
    horses breed
    in the extreme west,
from times past memory
    their drovers
    herd them east.

When spring and fall
    drive hard
    without remission
how then can wealth
    or rank
    resist?

Clear dews glaze
    the orchids
    in the marsh,
white hoar-frosts seize
    the level
    plains.

In the morning
    youth
    is soft,
late at evening
    age
    is hard.

We hold
    in perpetuity
    no grace.

That distant time
　　when I
　　　　was young
and laughed
　　and danced
　　　　and sang,

I wandered west
　　where the lights
　　　　burned bright
and mixed
　　in high
　　　　society.

But before the party ended
the bright sun went.

I spurred
　　my horse
　　　　towards home again,
inventorized
　　spent
　　　　years:

gold spilled
　　like sand
　　　　for junkyard goods;
steered north then
　　to the great
　　　　trunk road.

From this long
　　labyrinth
　　　　what out?

A month
    to go
inside this summer
    furnace.

Young leaves wilt,
    sweet resins sweat,
cool clouds stream
    across the sky.

Seasons no sooner
    in than gone,
moon and the hunting sun
    run on.

Pacing, pacing
    desolate halls,
grief knowing
    no friends

can yet desire
    true company
could cancel
    want.

Freshness arrives
    with the fall:
in the curtains
    crickets sing,

and mind turns
    fretful
as the heart
    grows dark;

words
    are withheld,
their sense
    suppressed.

Soft air
    unsettles
    these thin sleeves,
the moon sheds
    an unmitigated
    light.

Perched high
    the cock
crows in
    the dawn.

Carriage,
    take me home!

Morning,
    I scale
    the precipice;
evening,
    descry
    remote massifs.

Thorn-brush
    invades
    the plain below,
gregarious
    birds
    flicker up.

In solitude
    the phoenix
    dwells,
discharging
    the inheritance
    of its kind.

Heaven and earth
    are by a single tree
    conjoined;
account
    all other plants
    mere show.

Around,
    through forest
    undergrowth,
the fattening
    bindweed twines
    and thrives.

Deep grief
    constrains
        the will;
long pain
    is this continuing
        fear.

Does pleasure
    take?
        Sun
plunges
    down
        the west.

Crickets
    wither
        at the sill;
brief cicadas
    cry
        in the yard.

When heart
    and mind
        conflict,
who can
    discern
        true inclination?

Distant,
    a bird
        among the clouds,
I would
    shriek
        once.

Alexipharms for death
flourish
in paradise;
long flight
there brings
long life.

Would you
      shun grief?
Then eschew
      sense:

only the insensate
      never grieves.
Fall to no nets?
      Need no effects.

Pitiful eddies
      spin against
      the jetstream.
By light of suns
      the rainbow lives
      and dies.

Ashes
      for heart,
withered
      the frame;
can yet
      humanity
      attract?

I have achieved
      remission
      from the world;
how now
      without display
      efface?

peacocks
seem out
of place
and uneasy
here

large
rattling
tails
folded

eyes
all
neatly
stacked

like tenses
of some
complex
and irregular
verb tabled
in a grammar

could
should
would

or a hand
of cards

start day
mother day
love day
lost day
saint day
son day

the savagery
of calendrics
is extreme

doghunger
of the clock
gobbling up
its innocent
substrate

steel branch
and swivelling
leaf across
a jewelled
ground

i'm glad
you're here
old friend

happy we
can relive
again for
these few
days days
past

we'll drink
and talk
books
music
other friends
ourselves

so these
be days
remembered
in their turn

your glass?

he opened
a volume

something
white
fell
and
broke

he made
that book
his pet
fowl

nighttime
company
morning
breakfast

others
suggested
it was
a mirror

the egg
the moon's
reflection

i'm still
one
book
down

o tiny
universe

alongside
the many other
possible
universes
some of which
could easily
be ten
or a thousand
times more
vast

you are
small
pretentious
and a little
pathetic

i will
keep you
for later

barbarians
are bad
at walls

ours keep
them out

hordes
break
like a river
against
our bastions
and then
flow on

sweet
orchards
gentle
hounds
we have

the hands
of slaves
draw us
sweet
water
up

successively
each emperor's
doubles were
assassinated

then
himself

therefore
this stratagem

our latest
emperor
was chosen
secretly

no-one
informed
not even
the elect

it worked

somewhere
he lives
obscurely
on

quite
unaware
he is
a god

colour
is graded
with marvellous
precision

planes
cleanly
intercut

walls
grow
crystalline

charged with
superb light

thoroughfares
are painted
in the same
reddish clay
of which the city
itself is built

christ
and satan
haggle
above

examined
the water
with dragged
hooks

exantlated
bike-frames
prams and
sundry suspect
instruments

luxuriant
vegetable
incognito

that grand
canal
yielded no
body up

another time
it overspilled

skittered
down sunny
streets

slept
that night
in houses

they found
a bucket
filled
with tears

now they demand
whose property
is this

who so
decries
their state

no need
they say
not now

so why this
weeping
without owner
function
future
why these tears?

way too late
a key
is produced
the lock is fixed

the steed
at speed
is too far gone
already

coincidentally
a churn
has broken

lamentation
is pointless

there is
no crisis
no change
is imminent

i walked
through
the universe
of parmenides

was the only
thing
moving there

exhaled blood
stood
in mid-air

shattered
glass
hung
stilled
dust
in sunlight

truly

that world
is a complete
and exhaustive
omen
of itself

STILLSMAN

1 STILL THE HEART BEATS AS THE FIRST LIGHT BROACHES THE HORIZON HUNDREDS OF BIRDS STRIKE UP THEIR TINY BODIES FILLING THE AIR WITH FF MELODIES CUT WITH A SOLEMN OATH RECALL THE PATIENT ONE OSCAR C THOUGH A BED FULL OF BONES HAD ALWAYS ENJOYED EXCELLENT HEALTH PRESENTING NEVER BUT THE SHALLOWEST OF MALADIES AND BEING NEITHER ALCOHOLIC NOR SYPHILITIC GREW INTO A BRIGHT SHARP MAN POSSESSING THE THREE GIFTS OF HEARING SEEING AND OF JUDGEMENT AND HAVING PERDURED LONG IN TEXTILES HAD FOUND TRACTABLE ONE GROUP OF BIRDS THAT EASED HIS LIVING WEDDED BLISSFUL WITHOUT ISSUE WHILE THOSE TRAPPED VOICES METICULOUSLY CAGED IN MULTISTORIED CONSTRUCTS ABOVE VAST FLOORS BENEATH LOW BEAMS EXULTED AS HUMAN SINGERS CAN ONLY DREAM THIS COUPLE EVEN BEING VERY CLOSE AND HIS WIFE SOME YEARS THE YOUNGER VERY CULTIVATED TOO AND A PARTICULARLY GIFTED MUSICIAN WHICH TASTES SHE HAS INSTILLED IN HIM AS BARLEY ENGENDERS BARLEY THE LION A LION AND GOLD GOLD VIZ TWO VOICE BOXES ALLOWING HIM FREQUENTLY TO PERFORM DEMANDING SCORES WITH HER IN CONSEQUENCE OF WHICH SUCH A CREATURE CAN DO TWO DIFFERENT THINGS AT ONCE WITH ITS THROAT EVEN SING A DUET WITH ITSELF AND WHETHER ALONE OR WITH HER HE IS WELL UP IN BOOKS MISSES NOTHING AT ALL AND IT S OBVIOUS IN TALKING WITH HIM HOW THOSE LITTLE BIRDS PRODUCE SUCH BIG BEAUTIFUL SONGS WHEN THROUGHOUT THE AUTUMN MONTHS THE WHISPER OF THE WIND IN THE CORNFIELD IS FOREVER AUDIBLE AS THE GRAIN WHICH IS SOWN IN CORRUPTION BUT IS RAISED TO INCORRUPTION POURS INTO THE GIANT HOPPERS AND IS EXALTED FOR HE IS READ AND SENSIBLE WHAT INSTRUMENT CAN CRAFT SUCH MUSIC AT THE RATE OF SEVERAL THOUSAND BUSHELS AN HOUR AND THIS C HAS HAD EXCELLENT VISION ALWAYS SO THAT AGAINST THOSE MANY WHO WOULD ENTICE FRAIL BIRDS TO SING WITH FIBREOPTIC SCOPES DOWN THEIR SKINNY THROTTLES DURING HIS YEARS IN TEXTILES PURSUIT TURNED HABIT AS C MERELY DEMURRED YOU DO NOT RULE ME CLOUDS OF BLOOD WILL COME TO YOU THEN STRAINED HIS PEEPERS CONJURING NEW DESIGNS TO PLOT DOWN ON MM² GRAPH PAPER OR IN NUMBERING THE THREADS IN A FABRIC IN WHICH THE SHAPE OF THE MASS OF DAUGHTER CELLS THAT EMERGES IS USUALLY A BALL ALTHOUGH IN BIRDS SOMETIMES A SHEET AND HE HAD NEVER SUFFERED THE LEAST MIGRAINE THOUGH WITH UPPER VOCAL TRACT IMMOBILISED OR THE LEAST CEREBRAL PROBLEMS DISPASSIONATE EVEN IN AN EXPERIMENTAL AND WHOLLY ARTIFICIAL ATMOSPHERE BEFORE THAT FALL WHEN THEY PLOUGHED HIM DOWN AS MME C RELATED AND THE TASK OF TRANSLATION BEGAN 2 ONE DAY AS SHE WASHED FROM A SILVER VESSEL MOUNTED WITH FOUR GOLDEN

143

BIRDS WHILE ATTENTIVE TO THEIR BREATHING AND THE ACTION OF THE THROAT ON SONG HER HUSBAND ABRUPTLY ENDURED SEVERAL SHARP STROKES OF SENSELESSNESS IN HIS RIGHT LEG AS THE HUMID SEED BEGAN TO SWEAT FURTHER INTO DORMANCY AND IN THE SUCCEEDING DAYS FELT SEVERAL MORE SUCH BROADCAST ON WIDE PERFORATED FLOORS YET COULD THE WHILE RAMBLE ABROAD UNTIL GRADUALLY HIS RIGHT ARM AND LEG GREW WEAK AND HE CAME TO KNOW THAT HE COULD READ NOT A WORD THOUGH HIS SCRIPT AND SPEECH STAYED UP TO SCRATCH AND HE COULD TELL AS CLEARLY AS EVER FOLK AND THINGS ARRAYED SO THEN SUSPECTING THAT THE PROBLEM LAY WITH HIS EYES HE VISITED MY COLLEAGUE TO INTERROGATE THE THRUSH HOW IT CAN SING SO LOUD AND HE IN TURN REFERRED TO ME THIS SUBJECT IN WHOM WAS MANIFEST A MARKED AGRAPHIA ALONG WITH FADED AND COLORLESS VISION ON THE RIGHT ALTHOUGH TO UNDERSTAND YOU HAVE ONLY TO HUNT DOWN THE SYRINX THAT VOCAL ORGAN WHICH CONCEALS ITSELF BY CHANNELS DEEP BELOW THE NECK SO THAT WHEN READING AN EYE CHART C CAN IDENTIFY NO LETTER THOUGH HE CLAIMS PERFECTLY TO DISCERN THE SYRINX LYING LOW WITHIN THE BODY AND INSTINCTIVELY HE SKETCHES THE SHAPES OF THE LETTERS WITH HIS HAND BUT CAN T UTTER EVEN ONE OF THEIR NAMES FOR BIRDS DON T BREATHE LIKE YOU AND I HAVING INSTEAD AIR SACS TO PUMP AIR THROUGH THE LUNGS WHERE A SMOKELESS HEAT RISES FROM BELOW DRIVING THE DRENCHED AIR UP AND THOUGH MUCH MOVED HE CAN SCARCELY EVEN RECOPY THE LETTERS LINE BY LINE AS IF PLOTTING A TECHNICAL DRAWING SCRUTINIZING EACH STROKE TO REASSURE HIMSELF HIS DRAWING IS EXACT AND BONEDRY AFTER ONE CIRCADIAN CYCLE IT GOES IN STORE ENCLOSED BY ONE OF THESE SACS AS IT MUST DREAM UNDISTURBED FOR AT LEAST THREE WEEKS BEFORE TRANSLATION RECOMMENCE BUT STILL THE NAMES OF LETTERS REMAIN LOST TO HIM AS HE SAYS THE A IS AN EASEL Z IS A SERPENT AND P A BUCKLE THOUGH THIS WILL NOT APPEAR QUITE SO FARFETCHED GIVEN HOW CERTAIN INARTICULATE SOUNDS DO RESEMBLE PARTICULAR LETTERS AS THE TREMBLING OF WATER IS LIKE THE LETTER L THE QUENCHING OF HOT THINGS THE LETTER Z THE JIRKING OF A SWITCH THE LETTER Q &C BY AN EXACT OBSERVATION OF WHICH PARTICULARS IT MAY BE POSSIBLE TO MAKE A STATUE SPEAK SOME WORDS AND YET THIS FRAUGHT INCAPACITY FRIGHTENS THE PATIENT C BOUND SO NARROW IN A TANGLE OF MUSCLE NEAR THE HEART THE NUT SHAPED SYRINX PITEOUSLY TO CHAUNGE HIR SHAPE THE WATER NYMPHES BESOUGHT AND THINKS HE HAS GONE MAD SINCE WELL HE KNOWS THE SIGNS THAT HE CAN T NAME ARE LETTERS AND WHILE STUMBLING CAN TELL NUMERAL FROM LETTER REMAINS UNABLE TO READ HIS OWN COPIES OF THOSE

144

LETTERS THEY BEING QUITE IRREGULAR WITH Z REMADE
INTO A 7 OR A 1 AND THE STROKES FEEBLE OR OUT OF
PLACE HOW QUICK DO EVIL COMMUNICATIONS CORRUPT
GOOD MANNERS 3 CONSIDER THEN THAT WHEREAS IN
DUCKS CHICKENS PARROTS AND OTHER SUCH DOMESTIC
PRIMITIVES THE SYRINX LODGES IN THE WINDPIPE JUST
ABOVE THAT BRANCHING WHICH SERVES THE LUNGS
WHERE IT DRINKS DEEP UNTIL WATERLOGGED HE HAS
NO DIFFICULTIES REMEMBERING IN SUCH A COMPANY
AND THOUGH FEARFUL OF EXPRESSING HIMSELF
NONETHELESS SPEAKS FLUENTLY AND WITHOUT ERROR
CRYING OUT AT TIMES ATTEND GOOD NEWS NEWS FROM
THE LODGING THROUGHWAY FOR SHIPS MEN GLEAMING
ACCOUTRED BOASTING OF HURT GREAT DOWNFALL FAIR
FEMALE ON WHOM THE RED THREADWORK OF SLAUGHTER
HAS SETTLED ATTENDING TO SONGBIRDS SUCH AS
WARBLERS LARKS AND SPARROWS YOU WILL SEE A
DOUBLE STRUCTURE THAT SITS A LITTLE LOWER
STILL ONE PART WITHIN EACH DIVISION AND IF THEN
SHOWN ANY OBJECTS HE WILL NAME THEM STRAIGHT
OFF INCLUDING ALL THOSE MACHINE COMPONENTS
ILLUSTRATED IN A TECHNICAL INDUSTRIAL HANDBOOK
AND NOT ONCE DOES HE MANIFEST ANY PROBLEM
WITH RECALL IMMEDIATELY NAMING AND IDENTIFYING
THE PURPOSE OF ALL THE OBJECTS PICTURED IN THE
MANUAL UNTIL THEY SPROUT AND RAMIFY ABOUT HIM
SWEETLY ENACTING THEIR EXOTIC AND ACCELERATED
SPRING BUT THESE UNTIMELY GERMINATIONS POSED
NO PROBLEM FOR ONE AVIAN ANATOMIST WHO SHEW D
A WAY OF MAKING MUSICAL AND OTHER SOUNDS BY THE
STRIKING OF THE TEETH OF SEVERAL BRASS WHEELS
PROPORTIONALLY CUT AS TO THEIR NUMBERS AND
TURNED VERY FAST ROUND IN WHICH IT IS OBSERVABLE
THAT THE EQUAL OR PROPORTIONAL STROAKS OF THE
TEETH I E 2 TO 1 4 TO 3 &C MAKE THE MUSICAL NOTES
BUT THE UNEQUAL STROAKS MORE ANSWER THE SOUND
OF THE VOICE AS IT SPEAKS OUT ATTEND GOOD NEWS
OUR HORSES EXHAUSTED WE RIDE AND WE RIDE ON
UNCANNY STEEDS THOUGH ALIVE WE ARE DEAD GREAT
SEVERING OF LIVES LONG GORGING OF RAVENS BANQUET
FOR CROWS RATTLE OF SLAUGHTER WHISTLE OF EDGES
SHIELDS SHATTERED IN THE HOURS AFTER SUNSET
ATTENDING THE WHILE THE NIGHT SINGER IN THE
UNSTABLE RUSHES BROODS ON A CLUTCH OF STARS
4 BY THIS TIME THE ACROSPIRE HAS ALMOST BREACHED
THE HUSK AND THE STARCH IS SOFT AND CHALKY AND
WHEN YOU CAN WRITE YOUR NAME ON THE WALL WITH
THE EAR IT S READY WHEREFORE WHEN HE IS SHOWN HIS
REGULAR NEWSPAPER C RECOGNIZES IT CORRECTLY BY
THE LAYOUT BUT IS UNABLE TO MAKE OUT ANY OF THE
LETTERS IN THE HEADLINES JUST AS RESEARCHERS
HAVE LONG MADE DO WITH INDIRECT APPROACHES
SNIPPING THIS OR THAT MUSCLE AND WAITING TO
ASCERTAIN ITS EFFECT ON THE BIRD S SONG THOUGH

TEXTS ARE SOMETIMES EQUIPPED WITH WORD DIVIDERS WHICH SIMPLIFIES THINGS BUT IF THESE ARE NOT SUPPLIED THEN THE READER MUST EDIT HIS TEXT BY STUDYING THE REPETITIONS AND BREAK THE TEXT UP INTO ITS CONSTITUENT UNITS AS FOR INSTANCE IF THE PRECEDING PASSAGE WERE RUN TOGETHER STUDY WOULD SHOW THAT THE SEQUENCE THE FREQUENTLY RECURS AND MUST THEREFORE BE SOME COMMON WORD AND FURTHERMORE WHEN SHOWN ANOTHER NEWSPAPER WHOSE FORMAT HE DOES NOT KNOW AND WHOSE CONSTITUENT WOOD AND RAGS ARE PULPED BEYOND RECOVERY BY THE EYE C AFTER 5 MINUTES OF THOUGHT MISIDENTIFIES IT THOUGH AFTER A SPELLING LESSON OF 15 MINUTES HE IS FINALLY ABLE TO READ THE TITLE BUT IN ORDER TO RECALL THE LETTERS HE HAD SURGICALLY TO IMPLANT TINY DEVICES TO MEASURE AIRFLOW IN THE BRANCHED PASSAGES OF TWO SPECIES OF SONGBIRDS NAMELY THE GREY CATBIRD AND THE BROWN THRASHER SO THAT WHEN THEY RESUMED THEIR SONG A FEW DAYS LATER THEY SANG OUT CLEAR THE INTIMATE INJUNCTION HE WILL NOT KILL BIRDS AND C COULD TELL EXACTLY WHICH NOTES CAME FROM EACH OF THEIR TWO VOICES AND DRAW THEIR FORM WITH A GESTURE OF THE HAND WHILE NOT LOOKING AT THE NEWSPAPER BUT THE FURNACE RAGED AGAIN HALTING ALL DEVELOPMENT AND THESE INTIMATIONS HE STORED AWAY FOR A TIME 5 WHILE UNABLE TO READ THE PATIENT DOES COPY HIS NAME CORRECTLY AND WRITES FLUENTLY AND WITHOUT MISTAKE WHATEVER MATERIAL IS DICTATED TO HIM SINCE THE PAIRED SYRINX PROVIDES A VARIED TOOL BOX FOR CONSTRUCTING COMPLEX SONGS BUT SHOULD HE BE INTERRUPTED IN THE MIDDLE OF A PHRASE DURING DICTATION HE IS QUITE SHATTERED AND CAN T RESTART THOUGH THE THRASHER SING A TRUE DUET IN WHICH BOTH STONES GRIND AT THE SAME TIME TO ADD HARMONIC COMPLEXITY AND IF HE MAKES A MISTAKE HE CAN T FIND IT AND WHILE HE USED TO WRITE FAST AND FINE NOW HIS LETTERS GROW COARSE AND HESITANT FOR AS HE SAYS HE NO LONGER HAS CONTROL OF HIS EYES SO THAT ONE SIDE MIGHT FAVOUR A RISING NOTE THE OTHER A FALLING SAY SO THAT IN FACT RATHER THAN HELP HIM LOOKING WHILE HE WRITES DISTURBS HIM TO THE POINT THAT HE PREFERS TO KEEP HIS EYES CLENCHED AND WAIT WHILE SUCH AS THE BROWN COWBIRD SING RAPID FIRE BURSTS IN WHICH THE TWO SIDES ALTERNATE NOTES IN A STRATEGY THAT MAY ALLOW EACH TO GRIND EXCEEDING SMALL WITHOUT RAGGED TRANSITIONS THUS I AM KING OF YOUR FATHER S BIRD TROOP AND YOU MUST NEVER CAST AT BIRDS FOR THROUGH KINSHIP EVERY BIRD HERE IS NATURAL TO YOU UNTIL NOW I DID NOT KNOW THIS HE SAYS LOOKING AS HE WRITES MIXES HIM UP SO WHEN HIS DISORDER FIRST SET IN AND HE TRIED TO WRITE HE LAID THE LETTERS DOWN ONE ON TOP OF THE OTHER AND

THUS WHEN HE WROTE HIS FIRST NAME OSCAR HE PUT THE C ON TOP OF THE S NOW HE WRITES FROM MEMORY WHATEVER HE DESIRES WHETHER IT BE HIS OWN SPONTANEOUS WRITING OR AT ANOTHER S DICTATION HE CAN NEVER REREAD WHAT HE HAS WRITTEN EVEN ISOLATED LETTERS DO NOT MAKE SENSE TO HIM HE CAN ONLY RECOGNIZE THEM AFTER A MOMENT S HESITATION AND THEN ONLY BY TRACING THE OUTLINES OF THE LETTER WITH HIS HAND 6 WHEREAS IN MANY BIRDS THE TWO SIDES ACT LIKE THE TUNS AND KIEVES OF A SOUND SYSTEM WITH THE LEFT SIDE SPECIALISING IN LOWER NOTES AND THE RIGHT IN HIGHER WORKING TOGETHER TO PRODUCE SAY THREE REDS MUST NOT PRECEDE YOU WHERE RED DWELLS IT IS THEREFORE THE SENSE OF MUSCULAR MOVEMENT THAT GIVES RISE TO THE LETTER NAME AS THE CARDINAL THAT VIRTUOSO SWEEPS SMOOTHLY UPWARD FROM ABOUT 1 KHZ TO 7 KHZ LIKE THE FIRST ELEMENT IN A WOLF WHISTLE IN FACT HE CAN EASILY RECOGNIZE LETTERS AND GIVE THEIR NAMES WITH HIS EYES CLOSED BY MOVING HIS HAND THROUGH THE SCALDING WATER FOLLOWING THE OUTLINES OF THE LETTERS NOTING THAT AT ABOUT 3.5 KHZ THE SOUND SWITCHES SEAMLESSLY FROM LEFT TO RIGHT QUITE UNLIKE SPEAKERS C CAN DO SIMPLE ADDITION HOWEVER RECOGNIZING WITH RELATIVE EASE THE CRY OF OSSAR OSSAR THE HOUND BUT IS VERY SLOW READING EACH CHARGE POORLY SINCE HE CAN T RECOGNIZE THE VALUE OF SEVERAL NUMBERS AT ONCE AND THOUGH ONE CAN T SEE OBVIOUS DIFFERENCES IN THIS MISHMASH THAT DOESN T MEAN THEY AREN T THERE FOR WHEN SHOWN THE NUMBER 112 HE SAYS IT IS A 1 A 1 AND A 2 AND ONLY WHEN HE WRITES THE NUMBER CAN HE SAY ONE HUNDRED AND TWELVE ONLY SUPERFICIALLY IS HIS VOICE MONOTONOUS AND COMPOSED OF A SINGLE VOWEL AAA IN TRUTH IT STATES THE THOROUGH AND IMMENSE WEALTH OF THAT BODY BUT MUCH OF THE SPECIALISATION COULD BE ACCOUNTED FOR BY DIFFERENCES IN MUSCULAR FORCE APPLIED TO THE TWO SIDES SO PERHAPS IT IS A QUESTION REALLY OF GRANULARITY OF SCALE COLD WIND ACROSS A DANGEROUS EDGE NIGHT FOR DESTROYING A KING 7 AND C EMPLOYS HIS DAYS TAKING LONG WALKS WITH HIS WIFE AND COMPLAINS OF NO DIFFICULTY WALKING AND EVERY DAY HE DOES HIS ERRANDS ON FOOT ALONG A LONG FAMILIAR ROUTE FULLY AWARE OF WHAT S HAPPENING AROUND HIM HE STOPS AT THE WOODEN BACKS EXAMINES PAINTINGS IN GALLERY WINDOWS AND ONLY THOSE POSTERS AND SIGNS IN SHOPS SHOWING TOGETHER A BIRD A MOUSE A FROG AND FIVE ARROWS REMAIN SENSELESS COLLECTIONS OF SIGNS OFTEN EXASPERATING HIM FOR THOUGH AFFLICTED FOR FOUR YEARS HE HAS NEVER ACCEPTED THAT HE CANNOT READ THOUGH CAPABLE OF WRITING BEING WELL AWARE THAT CANARIES USE THEIR

DOUBLE SYRINX YET OTHERWISE THEY SING THROUGH THE LEFT AND INHALE THROUGH THE RIGHT SAYING FOR INSTANCE YOU ARE GOING AWAY YOU LOVE A FOREIGN WOMAN WHO BARS MY WAY TO YOU YOU WILL HAVE CHILDREN WHO WILL BRING YOU JOY BUT I AM SAD AND THINK ONLY OF YOU EVEN IF ANOTHER MAN SHOULD COME ALONG AND LOVE ME AFTER THEIR WALKS M AND MME C PLAY MUSIC TOGETHER UNTIL DINNER OR MME C READS TO HER HUSBAND BIOGRAPHIES OF MUSICIANS NOVELS OR THE LATEST NEWS AS FOR EXAMPLE OUR ENEMIES WILL SURRENDER TO US THEMSELVES THEIR LAND AND SEAS SINCE A MOUSE IS BRED IN EARTH AND SUBSISTS ON THE FOOD OF MAN AND A FROG LIVES IN THE WATER AND A BIRD IS VERY LIKE A HORSE AND THE ARROWS ARE ALL THEIR STRENGTH AND SUCH A STRATEGY IS POSSIBLE BECAUSE THE LUNGS CONNECT SO THAT A ONE SIDED INHALATION CAN FILL BOTH LUNGS WHICH DIVISION OF LABOUR IT IS RECKONED MAY HELP THEM DASH OFF LONG RUNS OF AS MANY AS 30 SHORT SOUND SEGMENTS PER SECOND YET TO AVOID SELFSTRANGULATION SOME SINGING CANARIES HAVE BEEN OBSERVED TO SNEAK A QUICK BREATH AFTER EVERY SYLLABLE SAYING UNLESS YE BECOME BIRDS AND TAKE TO THE AIR OR MICE AND BURROW INTO THE EARTH OR FROGS AND SEEK WATER YE SHALL FALL TO THESE SHAFTS AND FOR EVENING RECREATION THEY AGAIN PLAY MUSIC AND THEN SOME HANDS OF CARDS FOR HE IS INDEED AN EXCELLENT PLAYER PLOTTING HIS STROKES WELL IN ADVANCE AND IS IN THE HABIT OF WINNING SINCE SPEED IT SEEMS MAY BE THE CRUX AS FEMALE CANARIES PREFER MALES WITH FASTER SONGS AND THE MALES OF OTHER SPECIES MAY FEEL SIMILAR PRESSURE AS SWEETNESS TRANSLATES TO STRENGTH ONE MIGHT MAKE UP A TONGUE PALATE TEETH SOME LIPS A NOSE & SOME SPRINGS WITH MATERIAL & FIGURE LIKE THOSE OF THE VERY MOUTH AND IMITATE THE ACTION OF THESE ITEMS FOR THE GENERATION OF WORDS AND THEN ARRANGE THESE ARTIFICIAL ORGANS IN SOME CONSTRUCT FIXING IT UP TO UTTER NOT ONLY THE MOST PASSIONATE AIRS BUT ALSO THE MOST EXQUISITE VERSE WASHES OVER THE EASTERN HORIZON 8 SO AGAIN AND AGAIN C TRIES TO GET CERTAIN SPARROWS TO SING FASTER BY RECORDING WILD SONGS AND THEN HEATING THESE RETORTS OVER A FURNACE UNTIL SUBLIMATION EXPEL ALL NATURAL BREATHS FROM THE HEART OF THE RUN BETWEEN SYLLABLES WITH THE ROAR AS OF A GREAT WIND AND FROM TIME TO TIME HE GROWS AGITATED AND CANNOT ABIDE BUT PACES TO AND FRO USING THESE BREATHLESS SONGS LIKE THE AVIAN EQUIVALENT OF FINE PRINT IN RADIO ADVERTS TO CHARGE YOUNG SPARROWS THAT HAVE NEVER HEARD A NORMAL SONG AND TWICE HE FEINTS STRANGLING HIS WIFE AND THEN HIMSELF AFTERWARDS OBSERVING THAT THE BIRDS DO THEIR BEST TO COPY BUT CAN T KEEP UP

FOR MORE THAN A FEW SYLLABLES BEFORE STOPPING
AS IF TO CATCH THEIR BREATH UNTIL ONE DAY HE
OVERHEARS SOMEONE SAYING THAT THE SUREST WAY TO
A STILL HEAD IS TO JUMP OFF THE TOP OF A NOTABLE
MONUMENT WHERE IT IS HEARD AGAIN THE CRY OF
OSSAR OSSAR THE HOUND WHICH IDEA BECOMES FIXED
IN HIM AND HE SPEAKS OF IT WHEN EXCITED SO IT
BECOMES EVIDENT THAT EVEN A MINOR INCREASE IN
TRILL RATE GIVES RISE TO DISTURBANCE SUGGESTING
THAT SONGS IN THE WILD ARE AT THE EDGE WHEREUPON
ONE DAY HE GOES ALONE TO THIS MONUMENT AND
ASKS THE GUARD PERMISSION TO VISIT THE INTERIOR
BUT THE GUARD REFUSES TO LET HIM ENTER SAYING
THAT VISITS ARE NO LONGER PERMITTED SINCE TWO
PEOPLE COMMITTED SUICIDE IN THE SAME WEEK BY
JUMPING OFF THE TOP OF THE MONUMENT AH THE WORM
HE SAYS HAS BROUGHT THEIR SPIRITS LOW AND HE
WONDERED AGAIN AT THE BIRDSONG DECLARATIONS OF
WAR A PEOPLE DESTROYED THE RUIN OF A LODGING MEN
WOUNDED DESPONDENT A TERRIBLE WIND WITH LOSS OF
DEFENCES UNSUSTAINABLE PAIN MEANINGS FORGOTTEN
ALIEN HEIRS HARVESTS UNCUT A SHOUTING A SCREAM
BUT WHETHER THE BIRDS WHISTLE LIKE A KETTLE BY
FORCING AIR THROUGH A STRAIT VENT IN THE SYRINX OR
BUZZ LIKE A KAZOO RATTLING THE FLIMSY DRUM BESIDE
EACH OUTLET THE FIERCE UPSHOT MAKES THE SPIRIT
SAFE 9 FOLLOWING THIS PERIOD OF AGITATION HIS HAND
GROWS IRREGULAR AND MUST BE COOPED AND C WILL
NO LONGER INTERROGATE LIVING BIRDS BUT RATHER THE
EXCISED SYRINX OF A PRECIOUS FINCH WHICH NORMAL
MUSCLE TONE HAS DESERTED AND HIS ORIENTATION
REMAINS EXACT ALTHOUGH IN SPITE OF PATIENT LABOUR
HE CAN T ACCESS THE KNOWLEDGE OF THE LIVING BOOK
REVEALED TO THE EMANATIONS AS LETTERS WHICH ARE
NOT VOWELS NOR ARE THEY CONSONANTS THAT ONE
MIGHT MISREAD FOOLISHLY BUT ARE RATHER THE
LETTERS OF THE TRUTH WHICH THEY ALONE SPEAK WHO
KNOW THEM NOR CAN HE AGAIN DECIPHER A TABLATURE
BUT THAT SYRINX QUELLED IN BOND BETRAYS THE
ACTION OF THE HUMAN APPARATUS WHILE WHO KNOW
NOT THAT WHEREOF THEY SPEAK ATTEMPT TO MIMIC
VOICE WITH RIGS AND INSTRUMENTS YET HE CAN MASTER
UNFAMILIAR MUSIC EVEN REHEARSE THE INTACT BODY OF
TWO NEW WORKS AS HIS WIFE PLAYS FOR HIM SINGS THEM
WITH HIM FEEDING HIM THE KEEPSAKE WORDS SO THAT
AFTER A LITTLE PRACTICE HE CAN UNDERTAKE ONE IN
ITS ENTIRETY WITHOUT HER SUPPLYING THE SLIGHTEST
CLUE FOR EVEN A SINGLE SYLLABLE WHEREUPON TO
THEIR SURPRISE THEY OBSERVE THE SYRINX OPERATE
NOT LIKE A KAZOO OR WHISTLE BUT RESEMBLING THE
HUMAN VOICE AS IN SONG TAUT MUSCLES DRAW THOSE
TWO HEAVY FOLDS OF TISSUE THE INTERNAL AND
EXTERNAL LABIA INTO THE VAULT WHERE OUTRUSHING
AIR SETS THEM VIBRATING JUST LIKE HUMAN VOCAL

149

CORDS WHEN EACH SLIGHT UTTERANCE IS A COHERENT
THOUGHT COMPACT AS A BOOK AND HE RETAINS A
PERFECT NOTION OF MUSICAL RHYTHM AS THIS QUASI
KAZOO DOESN T AFFECT SOUND MUCH AT ALL SINCE
WHEN HE DESTROYS IT SURGICALLY PITCH AND VOLUME
ALTER ONLY IMPERCEPTIBLY 10 MIDWINTER SEVERAL
YEARS LATER DURING A HAND OF CARDS C DECLARES
THAT THE CHILDREN OF THE FATHER ARE HIS
FRAGRANCE AND IS AFFLICTED WITH PINS AND NEEDLES
IN THE RIGHT LEG AND ARM AND A GATHERING AND
INSUFFERABLE THIRST WHICH PERSISTS AS THE
DELICATE ETHERS GATHER AND RESOLVE AND WHILE
SOME COLLEAGUES FOUND AN INTRIGUING HINT THAT
THE SYRINX MAY RUN ON AUTOPILOT FOR A SPELL ONE
WENT IN SEARCH OF LIVING WATER FOR HIS KING SINCE
THE SONG OF THAT PRECIOUS FINCH SOMETIMES
CHANGES ABRUPTLY FROM A PURE TONE TO A NOISY
BUZZ AND BACK AGAIN AS HE LOVES HIS FRAGRANCE
AND MANIFESTS IT IN EVERY PLACE AND IF IT MIXES WITH
MATTER HE GIVES HIS FRAGRANCE TO THE LIGHT AND IN
HIS REPOSE HE CAUSES IT TO SURPASS EVERY FORM AND
SOUND AS HIS DETERIORATION PROCEEDS UTTERING
ONE WORD IN PLACE OF ANOTHER OR GARBLING SOUNDS
AS IT IS A CHILD WHO IS AGED IT IS GRIEVOUS HIS
SHORTNESS OF LIFE THOUGH HE CAN MIMIC EXTREMELY
WELL WHICH IS A HALLMARK OF A SYSTEM ON THE EDGE
OF CHAOS AND AN EXCISED SYRINX EXHIBITS THE SAME
SUDDEN SWITCHES WHEN AIR IS FORCED THROUGH IT AT
GRADUALLY INCREASING SPEEDS SO HE CAN MAKE HIS
WIFE UNDERSTAND WHAT HE WANTS THROUGH GESTURES
AND SIGNS OF AFFIRMATION OR NEGATION BUT HIS
WIFE GIVES HIM A PENCIL AND NOTICES WITH DREAD
THAT HE CAN NO LONGER WRITE TRACING ON THE PAPER
STROKES AND LINES WITHOUT ANY APPARENT SENSE
HA HA HA HA HA THIRST WHICH SUGGESTS THAT SIMPLE
CHANGES IN AIRFLOW RATHER THAN ELABORATE
ORCHESTRATION BY THE BRAIN MAY ACCOUNT FOR SOME
OF THE RICHNESS OF THE FINCH S SONG AND INDEED
MUCH OF ITS STRUCTURE IS MADE AT ONCE EXPLICABLE
BY REGARDING THE SYRINX AS MACHINE RATHER THAN
AS AGENT AND AS HE SIGHED WITH HIS BREATH THE
REEDES HE SOFTLY SHOOKE TREMBLING FAR OUT UNDER
THE CITY S COURTS AND THOROUGHFARES CHURCHES
TERRACES AND MARKETS FOR IF THE SYRINX IS THE
MOUTHPIECE OF A TRUMPET THEN A BIRD S THROAT
AND MOUTH PLAY THE PARTS OF THE TUBING VALVES AND
BELL AND RESONANCES HERE MODIFY ENORMOUSLY
THE CRY OF OSSAR OSSAR THE HOUND AS IT PASSES
THROUGH AND YOU MAY EASILY HEAR THIS EFFECT IN
HUMANS WHERE THE THROAT MOUTH AND LIPS FORM
ALL THE VARIOUS VOWEL AND CONSONANT SOUNDS
OF SPEECH AS WELL AS ISSUING THOSE MANIFOLD
DIFFERENCES IN TIMBRE THAT MAKE AN ABUNDANCE OF
SPECTRES AND CONSTITUTE THE ANGELS SHARE FOR

IT IS NOT THE EARS THAT SMELL THE FRAGRANCE BUT
THE BREATH THAT CAN SENSE SMELL AND ATTRACTS THE
FRAGRANCE TO ITSELF AND IS OVERWHELMED AS
THE CHARACTERISTIC FLAVOUR AND AROMA AND
BOUQUET ARE BORN AND NURTURED TO FULL RICHNESS
AND HE SHELTERS IT AND HOLDS IT WHERE IT CAME
FROM FROM THAT FIRST FRAGRANCE WHICH IS NOW
GROWN COLD 11 C S INTELLIGENCE REMAINS INTACT HE
UNDERSTANDS ALL QUESTIONS PUT TO HIM AND IS
ATTENTIVE TO ALL THAT GOES ON AROUND HIM HIS MIMIC
IS EXTREMELY EXPRESSIVE AND HIS PANTOMIME VERY
ARRESTING BUT WHO TALKS HAVING INSPIRED THE
SIMPLEST OF NOBLE ELEMENTS SHRILLS AS THAT LIGHT
MEDIUM CONDUCTS SOUNDS FASTER AND STRESSES
RESONANCES IN THE VOCAL TRACT AT SOARING PITCHES
THOUGH THE VIBRATION OF THE VOCAL CORDS CHANGE
LITTLE SO THE UPPER VOCAL TRACT ACTS AS A FILTER
PRODUCING PUREST TONES BY AMPLIFYING CERTAIN
UTTERANCES FROM THE SYRINX WHICH MADE A STILL
AND MOURNING NOYSE BUT AS MANY SONGS LEAP ABOUT
FROM FLAVOUR TO FLAVOUR BIRDS MUST CONSTANTLY
ADJUST THE FILTER TO ADMIT JUST THE RIGHT TONES
WHICH FILMED SPARROWS CORROBORATE AS SINGING
THEY MAY BE SEEN TO OPEN THEIR BEAKS WIDER FOR
HIGH NOTES THUS ABBREVIATING THEIR VOCAL TRACT
AND MAKING IT RESONATE AT A HIGHER FREQUENCY
THOUGH ALL BE ULTIMATELY BROUGHT TO UNISON AND
AT THAT JUNCTURE C REMEMBERING THAT HIS NIECE
CAME FOR LUNCH EVERY SATURDAY IN ORDER TO TELL
HIS WIFE THAT HE DID NOT WANT THE NIECE TO COME ON
SATURDAY DID AS FOLLOWS FIRST GOT UP WENT TO THE
DINING ROOM AND SET THE TABLE FOR THE THREE OF
THEM AS USUAL HIS NIECE HIS WIFE AND SELF HIS WIFE
UNDERSTOOD YOU WANT TO TALK ABOUT YOUR NIECE
SIGN OF APPROVAL SHE MUST BE WRITTEN TO LIVELY
SIGNS OF APPROVAL TELL HER THAT YOU ARE SICK
ENERGETIC SIGN OF DISAPPROVAL WRITE AND TELL HER
NOT TO COME LIVELY SIGNS OF APPROVAL AND OF
SATISFACTION ON THE PART OF THE PATIENT AT WHOSE
FEET FALLS STRAIGHT A NIGHTINGALE OF STONE AND IS
IT NOT SOMETHING IN A PSYCHIC FORM RESEMBLING
COLD WATER WHICH HAS FROZEN OVER EARTH THAT
IS NOT SOLID OF WHICH THOSE WHO SEE IT THINK IT IS
EARTH AND AFTERWARDS IT DISSOLVES AGAIN AND
SAVAGE IS THE ANSWER LET HER IN 12 IN SEEDS
ARE GERMS THAT HAPPENING IN WATER BECOME
FILAMENTS OR BETWEEN WATER AND EARTH ARE SLIME
OR WHEN THEY FIGURE IN EXALTED SITES MARK A
PROFOUND MUTABILITY AND SO IN AN EXPERIMENT YET
TO BE PUBLISHED RESEARCHERS IMMOBILISE THE KING
AND STRIKE OFF HIS HEAD ATTEMPTING THEREBY TO
REPLICATE AN EARLIER RESULT IN WHICH THEY HELD
SPARROWS BEAKS AT A FIXED GAPE BY CLAMPING THEM
FOR BRIEF PERIODS TO A BITE BLOCK AND AFTER A FEW

151

DAYS TRAINED THEM TO SING WITH THEIR BEAKS
CLAMPED SO THE MUTABILITY IS RECOVERED FROM FINE
TILTH AS CROW S FOOT ITS ROOTS LARVAE ITS LEAVES
BUTTERFLIES AND THIS THE BODY THOUGH SURE
ENOUGH THOSE BIRDS DID SING MORE LOFTY AND MORE
SHRILL WHEN HE POURED DRINK STRAIGHT INTO
THE PARCHED GULLET AND CRIED ALOUD WHO BRINGS
DRINK TO A KING DOES WELL WITH OVERTONES THE
STRAUNGENESSE OF THE WHICH AND SWEETNESS
OF THE FEEBLE SOUNDE FOUND ON THE MORNING OF
JANUARY 16TH 1892 THE CONSUMED C QUITE STILL
QUITE GONE QUITE PATIENT YET THE BUTTERFLIES
EVOLVE TO FRASS AND INFESTATION UNDERNEATH THE
FIRE AND SO LIKE EXUVIAE THAT THEY ARE CALLED
HOUSE CRICKETS WHICH AFTER A THOUSAND DAYS
TRANSLATE TO BIRDS KNOWN AS DRIED SURPLUS
BONES AND THE SPITTLE OF THE DRIED SURPLUS BONES
TURNS TO A FINE SPARGE WHERE IS THE PALATE SITUATE
AND THAT MIST FALLS AS MATRIX OF BITTERNESS AS
AUTOPSY REVEALED A RECENT LESION AND AN OLD
ALONG WITH EVIDENCE OF THE DESTRUCTION OF
CERTAIN FIBRE TRACTS DURING THAT FOREGOING
PERIOD IN WHICH HIS FACULTIES WERE MASHED AND
WASHED AND RECTIFIED AND THE DRAFF DID FATTEN
STALLED AND STABLE BEASTS BUT THIS BROUGHT ON A
FURTHER VISITATION WHEREFORE THOSE FRAGRANCES
THAT ARE COLD ARE FROM THESE BREAKDOWNS
WHICH PROVOKED WARMTH TO SUPERVENE AND DO
AWAY WITH ALL DIVISION SO THE COLD SHOULD NOT
COME AGAIN THAT THERE SHOULD INSTEAD BE IDEAL
UNISON AND THEY HAVE TAKEN HIS VERY HEART S BLOOD
AND DRANK IT ROUND AND ROUND WHERE YELLOW
WHIRLIGIGS SPRING OUT OF LOW WINES BLIND FLIES ARE
BORN FROM THESE CORRUPTIONS AND WHEN A LIVING
STRAND COUPLES WITH A DORMANT STEM START THINGS
WITH NO SENSIBLE NAME RECURRING AS PANTHERS
PANTHERS THEN AS HORSES HORSES MEN WHO WILL
RETURN DISPIRITED TO THAT GENERAL CONCOURSE
OR AT THE FINISH BREATHE BEYOND THE
SONET NOTES STONE TONES ONSET

say

how was
the table
set?

were the
knives
angled
just so?

did one dog
loiter here
another there
multitudes
yon?

what was
the appearance
of the man
in her bed?

i foresee
empires
laid waste

some forty
years later

approaching
the capital
they heard it
rattle and
wheeze
like a toy

once within
only with
difficulty
maintained
balance

on streets
still slick
and caked
with human
fat

or was it
twenty?

the griffin
guards
inestimable
things

gold
blood
the road
to salvation

gates
and doorways
are his preferred
habitat

his elaborate
iron
features
many hands
wear soft

he barks
at strangers

feeds the
incorrigible
appetite
of edifices

the team
he assembled
comprised
engineers
and mechanics

unique and
talented
individuals
all

who devised
new techniques
novel and more
efficient
systems

adapting
not only
proven
manufacturing
systems

but the methodologies
of grain mills
and slaughter
-houses

his dying
words

flesh
from his bones
be boiled

familiarly
inhumed

those urgent bones
to head
his remnant troops
in battle

this was not done

instead
flesh by bones
together
sweated

slow
remission

long
among
candles

workers
abandoned
work

athletes
left off
striving

the great
relaxed
their tyranny

men of leisure
stopped their
idleness

through corridors
and halls
and offices
state
functionaries
were arrested

and heard
the concrete
roaring

like
accelerated
water

Seriatim
    phoenix rise,
    flapping vast wings
to test
    the limits
    of cosmography.

Quick tilt
    of pinion:
    see them ride
the jet-stream
    and obliterate
    space.

They break their fast
    on windfalls
    of eternity
and sup
    exalted
    outside time.

Should these
    who haunt the blue
    fear nets?
Should such
    consort
    with primitives,

disclosing
    old
    vacuities,
trading
    coarse
    tags?

Dew stiffens
        into frost,
grass frays
        to husk.

What moral
        there?
What truth
        survives?

Bestride
        the stratosphere,
hold incorruptibles
        for intimates;

take pause
        unceasingly
                for breath.

Big talk
       vents indignation.
Procrastination
       wastes the heart.

Northwest
       I master summits,
southeast
       the wilderness.

Impenetrable jungle
       binds the land,
mountain ranges
       lift crests clear.

One thousand generations?
       A light snack to me!
Millennia?
       A momentary tremor!

Mudstone
       and jade
essentially the same,
       you say?

What end
       to weeping, then?

As a boy
    I grasped the sword
and easily outfenced
    my masters;

clean strokes
    sliced the clouds
till skill
    bred notoriety:

my sword chopped
    at the desert edge,
my horses drank
    peripheral chaos;

banners whipping
    the wind
joined gong and drum,
    my only music.

War is a sheer affliction,
    furious and sad;
boyhood
    bitter.

Clear bright
        low sun
slants up
        across my robe.

Dust-devils play
        at the perimeter,
cold birds huddle
        in economy of heat,

even monsters
        and exotics
congregate
        in time of need.

Our dynasts
        are snapped double
at the waist
        like virtuoso instuments.
Lost the habit
        of going straight?

Conspiring
        for vain honours.
Why wither further
        their sad hearts?

Swallows and wrens
        flicker and skim,
knowing better than to imitate
        the yellow crane.

The yellow crane
        beats its great wings
against the boundaries
        of the universe.

Try that just once?
        Forget return!

Exiting
    by the Eastern Gate
I sighted zones
    beyond the markets

where austerity has secured
    sufficiency,
and nature keeps the kingdom
    peaceable.

I was engendered
    in an evil age.
Frost stiffens now
    my rich brocades.

Foothills
    and summits
shiver in the chill
    air.

Under heavy
    clouds
darkness
    is thickening.

The migrant geese
    long gone
only the raptor
    shrieks.

Mode mood and time
    crash heart
to a white
    void.

At noon
    I dress
to greet
    most honoured guests.

What character
    of men are they?
Transient
    as dust.

Their robes
    are numinous,
and they address
    the void of things,

yet are abruptly
    gone.
Can such
    recur?

Polar
    cold
        marks terminus;
escape,
    even by ocean,
        has its end.

Our sun
    gone out,
        we stand
alone
    benighted
        and unkinged.

Better
    tend
        orchard
than forever
    watch
        your back,

yet see:
    even the vulgar
        sparrow
sits
    in someone's
        sights.

In a trice
    power slips
        the grasp;
armed men
    defile
        the grave.

Now loyalty's
        exemplars
                all are dead,
tears
        cancel
                face.

Give me
        a purebred
                from the riverlands,
let me
        traverse
                my range.

We, all impassioned,
     suffer
            grief;
feel no
     passions, know
            no grief.

If not already
     snarled,
            why covet
further
     traps
            and goods?

Minor
     vortices
            approach
the utter
     limits of
            the atmosphere;

in light
     the rain
            -bow
glitters
     and grows
            parched.

Heart
     to ash
            exhausted
settles
     in a ruined
            house.

Say, why
        should I
                experience
nostalgia
        for the forms
                of men?

How,
        rid now
                of all familiar
fixes,
        slough
                my self?

uh oh
here they
come

they'll hound
you and pound
you and hammer
you flatter than
pemmican

they'll process
the meat
of your dreams

reconstitute
soul with
machines

and you'll never
see anything
brighter than
coal

alas!

the sturdy
musculature
of our rustic
pursuers
flexed
onward
as ours
enfeebled

hearts in
pain
throats
howled
for
unobtainable
refreshment

objectively
the intervening
space
shrank

stilled with
exhaustion
one
comrade
fell

his
screams
encouraged
us

capture
of our
friend
afforded
breath

hope
arose
but fast
fell
back

persistence
exasperates

anxious
to hold us
surely
our enemies
split

one ran
straight on
the other
circled

we were
to be
between
two fires

narratives
neither
begin
nor end
with combat

innocence
begins
because
that's what's
been lost

closures
are private
solitary

mood
complex
with guilt
and duty

then
that's
fresh
meat
for dinner
said
the pig
to the
knife

several channels
tonight aired
footage

streets deserted
shuttered malls

rectangles
of freshly
turned earth
are visible

certain
voices
exist

it could not
be confirmed
whether
an atrocity
had in fact
occurred

an unidentified
vehicle is
approaching

this person
is alive
is afraid
this stranger
to me
is hurt
is not old
is prone
is not dead
this miscreant
etceteran
may be wronged
may speak
retaliate
is strong
is cruel
is dead
this

withdrew
through brick
coal sheets
of readings
counts
accounts

his mills
grind slowly

it is appointed
unto man

replaced twin
trepanned plugs
of bone

slipped back
into field
dressings

turned

and he
laid down
his life

they laid
them
regular
in rows

they brought
the worst
to tents

where skilled
men lopped
off what was
judged
unserviceable

a wagon
stood
behind

weighted with
superfluous
extremities

the legs
were shod
and stockinged
still

Break

Men hard at work,
Soon evanesced.
In earth they shirk,
Hard men at rest.

Sanctioned

The rivers
that irrigate
our dreams
run blood.

Our mountains
are serrated
with outcrops
of recall.

Those memories
we're told
we do
not have

strike root
and ramify
through fields
laid waste.

And yet
who cannot
curb rage
without cause

grief without
measure cannot
suffer suffering
will find

sad self outcast.
Suffering is
no longer
permitted.

The known edge of the known world

This boundary constitutes a permeable membrane. Between the unknown and the known is seepage; exotic phenomena zig and zag back.

We, on our side, may sometimes overhear the exit of the dead and caparisoned progeny of some minor god. The further reaches of the expansion of pi approach. Actuarial tables readjust themselves as they accommodate some data newly entered in this zone.

We suffer our compensatory losses. The inscriptions of Harappa have grown inscrutable. We have forgot what name Achilles bore when he lived among women. The identity of the Chittingden Hotel suicide, whose palm foretold her death, self-poisoned with carbolic acid, can no longer be retrieved.

The pattern of the primes appears congruent with the weave of that membrane, the very pattern of the flickering edge, the fidget of the infinite: visible / invisible.

Being no wiser than the next, I do not tabulate the world, or set my nets to catch what beasts may cross. The night is cold. I hug my fire and watch the news, wondering who next of those I love will quietly absent themselves.

keepsake

my memory she is so poor
say do you think of me
i lie on a high tower
listen down the earth through which
like darkness i balance like darkness
hear the many creatures glistening cold
just beyond the beam of light
i hear them dont switch off
my memory she is so poor

Utterance

crack the red wax open
read note readdress dispatch
so he enabled the correspondences
of others and to be so occluded
by the flux of words gave pleasure

as crescendo filled the branching
flickering the quilled exchanges
until one particular melody exhausted
silence and called out spontaneous
response:
            abyssal the flame hatches

in answer
the child
hears
heaven
is furnished

with wonders
never seen
on earth

void of familiar
vestiges

a sun
that barks?
fists
of clenched
water?
blonde
plaited
hearts?

no! all
too stale

absence
of contestation

the bell is
mercifully
undamaged

its familiar
note again
interrupts
women
at market
old men
at conversation
children
at their play

so they may
celebrate
this narrow
sea divides
their own good
settlement
from the main

men's bones
transit
our ports

bushels
in their millions
from the
mainland
theatres

and bones
of swift
steeds too

the grinders
meet
with ready
engines

to reduce
unto a
dusty state

farmers
anticipate
fertility
of fields

once encountered
you will always
know the tormentil

deep the mineral
soil is sealed
and red with iron

pines are dense
and acidlogged

fresh rains
run rancid
in the level
dark

and raise
the yellow
tormentil

Let the shrove-tide come
let it bring warm weather.

What weather?
Summer weather!

Rocking chair, billy goat,
what's in the ground?

Girls from the village,
they all got drowned.

Now they're kicking
up the daisies.

Now they're clicking
in the reeds.

Let the corn grow thick,
let the wheat succeed.

Bring us out the head
of a tik tak Turk.

How many burrows
did the little rabbits dig?

Pack the corn into the sack
and make it big.

We've run all the way
and we want some bacon!

Let the shrove-tide come
let it bring the summer sun.

With her brother
she walks in the garden,
the river wind
blows cold through them.

When the river wind
blows cold be sure
it weathers the weak,
the river wind.

I've nothing but a twig
to cut the quick water.
Please, quick waters, clear my way,
I'm looking for my old lost love.

I've nothing but a glass
nothing there but a flower.
O flower called forget-me-not,
why do you make me cry?

At the bottom of the garden
he harvests rosemary,
I gather sheaves
for my brown-haired man.

At the bottom of the garden
I lost one brass spur.
Go look for it, my love,
and if you find it make it chime.

Hey, brown-haired girl,
your bed looks wild,
and a brown-haired man
left his hat behind.

Hey, girl, fetch my hat,
fit it firm on my head,
so that bright moonlight
won't dazzle my eyes.

How happy the life of a horse! Hey!
Till the end when they mock him
and whip him and kick him,
and for Purgatory sell him to gypsies.

Thirty years I served one man,
hauled his harness like a colt,
now I'm old I'm down and done for,
corn-stalks hurt my gums.

Smiths and farriers rot in hell!
Your tackle was the death of me,
they broke my head, they stole my skin,
now sheep-dogs sniff my meat.

The cart's here, I must go.

Ferryman, ferryman,
take me across,
carry me safe in your boat.

No time for goodbye
to my father.

Ferryman, ferryman,
take for the cost
this ring from my hand.

No time for goodbye
to my mother.

Ferryman, ferryman,
take for the cost
these pearls from my hair.

No time for goodbye
to my friends.

Carry me into the strange land.

New father, new mother,
how can I please him,
how can I please her?

Lie down late, rise up soon,
that's how you'll please him,
that's how you'll please her.

Lay down late, rose up soon,
still couldn't please him,
still couldn't please her.

Make the bed, wash the flags,
that's how you'll please him,
that's how you'll please her.

Made the bed, scrubbed the flags,
still couldn't please him,
still couldn't please her.

Set the fire, boil the pot,
that's how you'll please him,
that's how you'll please her.

Set the fire, boiled the pot,
still couldn't please him,
still couldn't please her.

Boil the pot, scald them blind,
that's how you'll please him,
that's how you'll please her.

The derelict mill
has a rafter of oak.

Perched on that rafter
half-woman, half-owl.

Is it grieving you are,
half-woman, half-owl?

Can't you see how I weep,
don't you hear how I grieve?

In my home I clean forgot
my ornamented couch.

On that couch I clean forgot
my loving man.

By that man I quite forgot
my flickering lamp,

In the light of the lamp I quite forgot
my crying son.

Beside my son I quite forgot
I set down my tin box.

In that box I quite forgot
my knotted loop of hair.

If I had it now
I'd jump like a horse.

If I had it now
I'd spin in a ring.

I was called
to come home.

My loving man,
he called me home.

My crying son,
he called me home.

I'd go home
if I could.

I'd go home
but I can't.

I'd go home
but shame
prevents me.

Father, come home,
my mother's not well.
Hold on, daughter,
I'm dancing.

Father, come home,
my mother's being shrived.
Hold on, daughter,
I'm dancing.

Father, come home,
my mother is dead.
Hold on, daughter,
I'm dancing.

Father, come home,
my mother's being waked.
Hold on, daughter,
I'm dancing.

Father, come home,
my mother's being buried.
Hold on, daughter,
I'm dancing.

My horse is shod
with shining brass.
The teacher's daughter
is delicate.

Her feet are shod
in soft red plush,
I go poor
without return.

Set to mind
my father's herd
I fell asleep
in the gap.

At midnight
when I woke
that whole field
stood emptied out.

The train runs slow
though the wheels spin fast,
with a fresh consignment
of recruits.

Three brown-haired girls
with sweet soft words
try to get the engine-driver
let their lovers go.

These recruits, dear ladies,
can't go free
till their three years
time is served.

— Be strong, my love!
— Oh, Captain, I grow weak.
— Ay, but three years more
will make a man of you!

Hey! Those guys
in the market
shortchanged me.
Took my mule,
took my barrow,
took my sister's sack
and my sick
brother's crutch,
hey ho!

Hey! Go
to the next house
beg for bread.
What did they give, son?
Just a penny, dad.
Put it in the bag, son,
it'll buy strong drink,
hey ho!

Hey! Go
to the next house
beg for bread.
What did they give, son?
Eggs aplenty, dad.
Curse those eggs, son,
throw them at the wheels,
and watch that bag
so no one steals it.
Ho, hey ho!

Katy falls sick
by the walnut trees,
by the hazel trees,
by the nut-tree grove.

Her mother asks her
where's the pain.
Not my head,
not my heart.

My head
doesn't hurt,
my heart
doesn't hurt.

Mother have my heart
cut out,
my calling heart,
my joy.

Have it cut out,
pack it up in a case
and carry it safe
to the shop.

When they ask you
what you sell,
say it's Katy's calling heart,
her joy.

Circum dadarunt
megamitus mortis
dolores in fergis
circum dadarunt me.

Why did you knock back
brandy and camphor?
Those two don't belong here,
the curate and cantor.

(Then the cantor intones:)

This poor God-help-us-case,
this unmarried misery,
choked on his cabbage,
and goes to his grave.

His twins Charlie and Jehr
still run with the herd,
so God bless his straw bed
and the worms at his head.

In the ditch beyond,
there's a dead nag now rotting
with a hole in his chest
for the devil to hide in,

Amen!

Shackled ankle
fettered wrist,
dark wears
eyes waste.

Glancing viper
spare me light,
rattling irons
ring my night.

Four walls
firm friends,
cold stone
my bed.

Hey, Jack, how come
I rot, not you?
You the horse-thief,
mine the grief.

Heard of the famous
county pen?
I'm in cell-block
number one.

First by number,
worst by name,
may God afflict
the architect.

Crying mothers
crowd
the stone
surrounds.

Hush, my mother,
this is fate,
from each family
one wretch falls.

The peacock
is merciful,
screams
on the stone.

Brings us
a sip
to wet
our lips.

Convicts, convicts,
on your knees,
beg to God
to be released.

O Lord, O Lord,
sweet Lord, my God,
when is my time
to be reprieved?

I'll be reprieved
when a single grain
yields up a hundred
sheaves of wheat.

The cedar dies
from the top,
the prisoner dies
in the pit.

Of nine strong bonds
I've worn out eight,
the ninth one
wearies me.

examine
your own
features your
distinguishing
characteristics

are you so
sleek?

pelt
cannot
remain
intact
eye
always
bright

living
dims

here we
enhance
the vestiges
of animation

with wire
and common
glass
we mend
broken
beasts

cut a god
the wound
destroys
the knife

slaves
are easier

simmered
honey
and red
flower
of copper

smeared
generously
the green
wound

discharge
watery
and thin

she died
in the night

she was
a barbarian

they offered
hospitality
to our gods
who unaccountably
decamped

city
groves
and temples
voided out

our prayers
decrees
and formulae
blind
breath

terror
and forget
fulness
succeeded

gods
and salt
trade
gone

who is to
pity us?

long
beards
ragged

without shoes
or stockings

clothes and
accoutrements
fragmented

heads
swathed
in old
rags

weapons
covered
with rust

not a few
from toil
and fatigue
quite blind

yet were
we not to be
despised

when i fail
to find
what i am
looking for

what is it
i want
to find?

a ghost
is incorporeal
outrage

some drifting
populations
are attracted
by unseen
concentrations

painstakingly
the wound
pursues
the knife

Sursum Corda

Like the encyclopaedia,
that instrument of our enlightenment,
this lens collects and concentrates.

A scattered world
is figured here
in neatness like a parlour.

Experience, if you please, the satisfaction
of it: breath, severance, memory,
the active street, the individual space

ranked here for safe inspection.
In this you get many for the price
of one. The consumer is empowered.

Alexander fevered and died
of his conquests — why should we
suspect the force of words?

smite to separate

smite retain caress hoodwink abide separate
hold anthracite fool compress sever cockeyed
absurd vestibule coal endeavour squeeze old
hall bird try stroll obsolete chevaux-de-frise
let high bluejay sweet hike highball
great pet frangipane stay drink strike
smite retain caress hoodwink abide separate

fissuring
faulting
jointing

crack
thundifferentiated
to an interlock
of vaults
boxes
rooms

rivers
their
walls

stone
furniture
stone
air

diviners
sense
the strike
or dip

when over
charged
a perched
table pitches

afflicting
property

overwhelming
thirst

torrential
penetrates
and rots
the sight

starved
memory
lives off
its store
and wastes

letters? no
correspondence

change? yes
necessarily
it occurs

subdued
of little
consequence

am
out of
harm's
way
here

stone
streaming
glass
opaque

grown
our familiar
companions

bleeding
after us
a sand
too fine
for sand

like aftermath
of fierce
localized
conflagration

and asking
in return
only the residues
of calculations

the waste
detritus
of approximations
to sustain them

i have
licked
mica
out of
granite
glint
from silver

yet
thirst
persists

my own
blood
too salt

never
could
alleviate

i lie now
where the
great river
suffers
crushed by
dispassionate
turbines

suck
its juices

the crying
goes on
and on

it might
be comforted
by some
attention

relief for
hunger
thirst

the warmth
scents
sounds
of a familiar
body

for lack
of these
uninterrupted
simply
it continues
on and
on

icy rivers
evaporate

the inertia
of the dunes
is illusory

one finds
the parched
timbers
of a town

exposed
in the
treacherous
drift

a forgotten
script
surfaces

before
it can
blossom
into voice
black
hurricane
obliterates

first the
universal
solvent
was discovered

not until a split
second later
did the search
commence
for the absolute
container

bottles glasses jugs
aluminium buckets
safes courts
cells dissolve

degrading
selflesh tumbles
through the
distressed
spaces

court
tombs
constitute
our earliest
examples

local sites
exhibit small
side chambers

transepted
galleries

only the
largest
slabs
remain

fallen
displaced

smaller stones
purloined for
nearby walls
or roadworks

the ideal form
exists
in imagination
only

Elements

```
fire      in     the    wood
smoke    wind    bird   song
wood     for     the    trees
flame    earth   beast  stream
ashes          to       ashes
nest     blade   light  rock
trees    for     the    wood
web      rain    shade  speech
wood     in      the    fire
```

Dramatis Personae

This hot,
    utterly jubilant
        baker,
            as I indicated, was investigating

Some bright,
    yet sufficiently despondent
        nurse,
            who without difficulty

Had solved
    a laughing
        (but a bit inebriated)
            carpenter's mega-

Problem,
    and self-destructed completely
        without any warning. "Oh maid!
        Childish

Smiling
    light of my life!"
        "That's quite enough,
            thou tepid artisan,

Though on the lam
    still harking back."
        Whereupon a slightly dim
        transient

Priest declaimed:
    "Fire of my loins!
        Life-sized
            exorbitantly playful

Aviator
of my passionate sky!
I advance, a middle-aged
adequately screaming

Living man,
occasionally frigid,
now and again chatting
a little."

For example:
"Oh female;
dark, strange,
almost hidden entirely,

Somewhat minuscule
girl,
pranking hither and yon,
and at this point

Barely old."
A boy begging
familiar
goods.

Causes of Affects: A Sentimental Retrospect

From the Heart of the Settlements we are now got into the Affections; the Keepers of these are a very extraordinary Kind of Fellows, they drive up their Hordes athletically, and they had need do so, for their Feelings are near as wild as Deer; an Affection generally consists of a very large Compound or Holding in the Past, with about four-score or one hundred Classifications, inclosed with strict Criteria and divided; a small Inclosure they keep for Love, for the family, the rest is the Privacy in which they keep their Domestic Rages; but the Manner is far different from any Thing you ever saw; they may perhaps have a Stock of four or five hundred to a thousand Head of Feelings belonging to an Affection, these disperse as they please in the Great Past, where there are no Inclosures to stop them. In the Month of March the Things Forgotten begin to drop their Domestic Rages, then the Affection Master, with all his Men, rides out to see and drive up the Things Forgotten with all their new fallen Domestic Rages; they being weak cannot run away so as to escape, therefore are easily drove up, and the Moments of Sadness and other Feelings follow them; and they put these Domestic Rages into the Privacy, and every Morning and Evening suffer the Things Forgotten to come and nourish them, which done they let the Things Forgotten out into the great Past to shift for their Recognition as well as they can; whilst the Destructive Spasm nourishes itself upon one Occasion of the Thing Forgotten, the Woman of the Affection is controlling one of the other Occasions, so that she steals some Control from the Thing Forgotten, who thinks she is giving it to the Destructive Spasm; soon as the Thing Forgotten begins to hunger, and the Destructive Spasm grows Strong, they mark them, and let them go into the Past. Every Year in September and October they drive up the Market Impulses, that are promising and mature, and dispatch them; they say they are promising in October, but I am sure they are not so in May, June and July; they reckon that out of 100 Head of Feelings they can dispatch about 10 or 12 Impulses, and four or five Things Forgotten a Year; so they reckon that an Affection for every 100 Head of Feelings brings about 40 pounds Sterling per Year. The Keepers live chiefly upon Control, for out of their Vast Hordes, they do condescend to tame Things Forgotten enough to keep their Family in Control, with Comfort, Curds, Politeness and Amusement; they also have Flesh in Abundance such as it is, for they consume the old Things Forgotten and lean Domestic Rages that are like to go. The Affection Men are hardy People, are almost continually athletic, being obliged to know the Haunts of their Feelings.

You see, Sir, what a wild set of Creatures Our Civil Men grow into, when they lose Society, and it is surprising to think how many Advantages they dispense, which our near industrious would be glad of: Out of many hundred Things Forgotten they will not give themselves the trouble of controlling more than will maintain their Family.

You could hear
        a pin
                scrape,
as if the company
        were a dove.
                "Take charge

of the hoard,
        record
                each unit
of beauty
        to calm
                the storm."

As if that might
        bridge
                division.
As well pretend
        this cloth
                were the world-soul.

"Detachment
        is a quiescent
                load,
and safer
        than the touch
                of seduction."

Back the serene
        hawk
                wings.
Even his
        mastery
                is contingent,

the way that
 out of gold
  the cold light
fires detail
 into illusion
  of life.

"As well search out
 a hole
  and start
already the body's
 settlement.
  A shell

of words
 makes
  a chancy
outfit."
 I felt meek then,
  yielding.

A snipe
 wing
  (can't you recognize it?)
had rotted.
 How, again,
  put trust

in what's
 so fleet?
  Strike
pieces
 from the wind?
  "My finger hasn't

a properly
    tranquil
        accommodation
of blood.
    Who then am I
        to command

even cottons,
    who
        to touch
the soft
    formation
        of effects?"

De Iron Trote

As man, in deep and level sleep, periodically draws a long inspiration, song is learned and figured in the brain. Think of the way a musical box, wound up, potentially represents a slow or lively air.

Clothes, however thick, diminish little the sonorities of breath. Touch the stop and the air sounds out; send an impulse along the proper afferent nerve and voice starts on song. Succussion, too, may raise a splashing sound much like the respiration, voice, and tinkling. Odd.

Garments of silk, or thin dry wool, also give rise to a noise calculated to cause error, sometimes mitigating the production and carefully controlled cropping of live creatures for high ends. Else, from every corner of the woods and glens see them come creeping on their hands, for their legs cannot make fast, as in humans the larynx migrates down the neck since the age of eighteen months, from which arises the sound of voices. In time these come to speak of a political meeting, of market shares. Someone tells of a woman who murdered her lover. "A chauffeur kills his wife," says another. All teetotallers like sugar. No nightingale drinks wine. Go figure.

The respiration of the plumpest child is louder clothed than of the thinnest adult frame stripped down. The throat is delicate and worthy to be protected. Says who? Whose voice? What proof is there these brutes are other than a superior race of marionettes, which eat without pleasure, cry without pain, desire nothing, know nothing, merely simulating true intelligence, for all it has been said that when emotions stir within, they take form in words?

To be included here is the agopithecus, an ape-like goat whose voice is very like a man's but not articulate, sounding as if one did speak hastily with indignation or sorrow, as here, where one such encounters in the woods a boy: "What's that you have?" The boy holds it out. It is a toy, a bear. A teddy bear. The boy's eyes are large, but without expression. "I don't want it, keep it." The boy hugs the bear again. A house takes fire. Later comes the writing of authorizations and designs on shop window tickets, and of inscriptions too private to allow printing.

In women who are both grown up and fat, the respiration is often audible with great force, even through the breasts. When your raptors are at fault, prevent all speech: let such as follow them ignorantly and unworthily, stirrup all aloof, for whilst such are chattering, none will hunt. *A-propos,* Sir, a politician will say: "What news from America?" *A-propos,* "Do you think both the admirals will be tried?" Or, *a-propos,* "Did you hear what has happened to my grandmother?"

Such rustling sensations are nothing else than a purring-thrill, and when this co-exists with the sound of the bellows, rasp, or file we may be assured others will soon resemble anatomies of death, like ghosts crying out of their graves, and will eat the dead carrions, happy where they find them, and the very carcasses they spare not to scrape back out of their deeper sleep.

Ticket writers may proceed to designs for posters when they can name their own figure. The illusion of experience, as a rule, begins by filling in provided letters with paint, and later gets on to the proper writing and lettering. Attendance at technical classes would be useful in order to bring up a good style of writing with some originality.

A dull but strong sound like that produced by a file on wood has something harsh in its sound. So, other boys start as heaters, then exercise as rivet-carriers, holders-up, anvil-hands, and lastly platers. Hear the whizzing sound of the left auricle.

Caution: Boys are often required to stand inside the chamber, as supporters, while the men pierce, and then hammer it outside, and deafness is apt to result. I found one who had abandoned his laborious occupation, and gained an easy place as servant to a priest.

Work with letters may be done sitting without difficulty and is quite suitable for cripples. The trade is not a large one.

In order
        to succeed
            a boy
should have a
        taste
            for drawing

ties
        with wild
                designs
unrestrained
        by thumb-
                tacks,

and thereby
        put by
                for a secure
old age
        a tidy
                sum,

for he might yet
        have to pit
                a warrant
'gainst a blackjack,
        drag
                his doll

with teats
        hitched,
                not as the fastidious
permit,
        but heaved
                in fullest view

by a snurting,
        as if some crack
                ensemble
had outrageously
        let
                fly

against all
        refined
                precedent
when we would have
        some prudence
                hinder her.

"Rear
        exit and begone,
                my own
exhibitionistic pet!
        Let's catch
                the track

will lead us
        to our train
                of state,
then venerably
        process."
                "A chorus

we must have
        to free ourselves
                of drills
and drawbacks,
        trials
                and tribulations."

Experience
      will seize
            the way.
Don't fix
      what ain't yet broke.
            You've heard it's true

that by a snifting
      clack
            the air
is expelled
      from the
            pickle-pot.

The Peacock's Tale

The costume of the people is so wretched that, to a one who has not practiced such visitations, it is almost inconceivable. Shoes or stockings are seldom to be seen on children and often not on grown persons, so yet they stand shod only in the plush of their red bogs, making unsteady verticals.

The rags in which both men and women are clothed are so worn and complicated, that it is hardly possible to imagine to what article of dress they have originally belonged. Duds, threads, fatigues and once-fancy hand-me-downs step out in parallel, all swaddled in knots, bedizened in glad rags; wardrobes run down past the least coherence.

It has been observed that these sheer beasts never dismantle themselves of their clothes when they go to bed; but the fact is, that not only are they in general destitute of blankets, but, if they once took off their clothes, it would be difficult to put them on again. Is not this a terrible way to be naked: wanting spread or comforter, however mute; to lie in envy of the gravel under grass?

Thus, their habit is worn day and night till it literally falls to pieces; and even when first put on, it is usually cast-off fragments; for there is not one subject out of ten who ever gets a coat bespoke, but chaff away instead their little means at hazard, where at last, exposed by numbers and for lack of other stuff, they pawn the nails of their fingers and toes, with shirred and smooth and shaggy, even to their kelder and dimissaries. That's the way they walk in view: tender and fractious, unsheltered and exposed, while yet not wholly detached, as the moth waits famished and the needle rusts.

239

God!
    Just think
        of all those pianos
standing
    with their white
        tusks

splayed
    in anticipation of toccatas.
        So toe
that foxtrot,
    glide
        your finery,

and be glad to be in the first
    frush
        and you'll get by.
Chaffer away
    as the spitfire
        blooms

run
    above you.
        Untache yourself, would you,
and get up
    on that stone
        like a bloody peacock!

Get yourself into
    the swim.
        Sure, any animal
is "disfigured"
    when disrobed of its
        hide,

"and cold too,"
        as the motley
                sow
remarked to her farrow.
        Unbrace yourself there
                in front of

the warmth.
        Let that uniform
                out a loop
and join us in the next
        tranche
                laundered.

The bunny hugs
        its burrow
                as the addict
does his coupon.
        You can never have too much
                exposure.

But I cannot lie!
        Bleach
                leached once
even into my livery,
        quite stemmed
                that old cashflow.

I'd a damned sight sooner
        break
                into a pavan
than go higgling
        with those demons.
                Let the cast of them

go splat
    and which of you would raise
        a finger
to get out?
    Climb past these
        unmentionables let you.

The human
    is a thing
        who
walks
    around
        disintegrating.

always
different
isn't it?

even though
you sketch
the structure
beforehand

even after all
childhood
spent aloft
or dreaming
outbursts
of limbs

branching
surprises

and always
from the highest
twig
the redbreast
calls you
sweetly
up

o certain
exotic
lozenges

yellowish
or blue
or purple

were most
prized

they were
traded
in the yard

a thriving
market
beyond
feather
bone
or tooth

two songs
one blue

kisses
for yellow

gold
without
measure

light
astral
obdurate
implacable

light
the strongest
biggest
thing

crouch
down here
beside me
light my pet
my little dog
my doll

and i will
caress
untangle your
wild hair
and you will
be my
friend

On the Island

here six foot
    or less divides
the grass floor
    from the firmament
of branch leaf
    subtle lichen

pages on music
    on colour
pass under
    my blind hands
birds sing the dog
    sleeps on

this space we occupy
    it ages
and we with it
    the stems bend
before my skin
    feels the air shift

from inside a womans
    voice singing
the sun moves round
    all precipitation
is blossom
    the dog stirs

whitening under sweet snow

(west tisbury, martha's vineyard,
31.5.03)

The Appearance of the Face

At the slaughter-house the head is split and the brain excerpted, leaving tongue and eyes in situ. The whole or half head is then boiled for two to three hours to ready it for table. The appearance of the face is important and an attractive expression desirable, so much so that a peaceful smile can double the price of the cut.

Varied life-courses arouse variety of taste: some favour the nose, others the ear, others yet the tongue and jowl, or perhaps "the ladder" as we call that corrugated place, the palate, but who would dispute the eye-muscle as most toothsome of morsels?

At table, parents, sibs, and gentle visitors wrestle for this succulent thrum, which is extracted by finely slipping one's baby finger behind the eye and withdrawing the band of soft meat.

Frequently the head is eaten cold at tea-time, sliced and served with mustard as centre-piece of a classic old Meat Tea. Alternatively, it may be sliced and fried on the pan with lard or dripping. Truly, a dish to feed a king!

mission

this facility
delivers always always deals
promotes & grows
nourishes fosters rewards

this division
ennobles & is exalted
demands yet provides answers
listens as it instructs
preserves controls enriches

this corporation
maintains & is maintained
its power
is the source of measure
is the home of speech
is the conflux of goods
& it gives strength
to whom it will

this system
is capital & it
exceeds all bounds
outruns comparison
evades examination

it numbers us
among the wise
& we depart
from those poor ignorant

choose
positive
terms

middle-aged
teller
found new
fulfillment
working
with the
disabled

operator
learned
three foreign
languages
now enjoys
vacationing
abroad

say

engage
sympathy

gun-shops
to be notified

similarly
police and
bar-owners

remember
these are
surplus

were the
attraction
so simple
would not
manifold
suns suffice?

fritter on metal
and bright
devices when
constellations
offer?

no!
soar

break
enter
stars

or for thieves
do the dark
bands
resemble
too closely
a cage?

the enclave
the exchanges
the unseeing
the transitions
the missing
the unravelling
the dwindling
the sigh
the slight
the sheeting
the switch
the stocktaking
the returns
the accounts
the breakdown
the loss
the excesses
past caring

she pours
milk
from jug
to dish

explain
to me
the odd
tenderness
of the gesture

a closed
liquid
transmitted
between
hollows

what colour
is the interior
of milk?

i shadow
your dust
hating
the light

application
of this
compound
to experimental
animals
leads to an
irreversible
situation

the animals
run round
in circles
describing
a circle
with their
heads

without en
-dangering
their lives

psychosis
is
unnecessary

such
substances
we call
disturbers

limb
trunk
extremity
dreaming withdraw
through populated
time

sharp educates
the reach

glare tutors
eye

you stepped
carelessly?

no matter

stone
will teach

blaze
admonish

tongue
castigate

raised fist
remind

go show
your grand
-mother
the doll

earth
fabric
mother
utensil
frugality
and balance

is a cow
with a calf
a wagon
is the markings
on things
is the many
things
the grasp
of things

in respect
to soils
is the
black
kind

with heaven
we begin

round is
the sovereign
father
jade
metal
coldness
ice

is pure
red
is a fine
horse
is an old
horse
an emaciated
horse
a piebald
horse

and is
fruit
of the
tree

Capital Accounts

Through this long peace
arterial routes
intersect
with narrow lanes.

Beasts of burden,
black and white
drag coaches
of sweet-smelling wood,

and jade-inlaid
sedan chairs
cross recross
the town.

Past celebrity glitz,
old money dens,
golden accessories
circulate.

Dragons gnaw
rich canopies
glinting
in the early sun;

phoenix vomits
glittering lace
under crimson
evening clouds.

One stretch
of gossamer
encompasses
the trees;

assemblies
of magnificent birds
unify the groves
with song.

•

Birdsong
unifies the groves,
moths flicker
through the thousand gates.

There are emerald trees,
silver terraces,
colours
you don't have names for.

Forked galleries
with window bays
assume the form
of leaves,

and ridge tiles
linking towers
are phoenix wings
at rest.

The Corporation's
ornamented halls
rival
the sky,

and the Executive's
immortal works
overreach
the clouds.

In front
of the high-rises
not a single face
you know.

Imagine!
On the streets
you encounter
only strangers.

•

What about her,
who puts on airs
facing
the purple mist?

In the past
she danced,
oh
how she danced!

It's like she's blind now
in one eye;
would another
cure her mind of death?

It's like she's lost
one of her arms;
and she's sick of dying
bit by bit.

•

She's sick
of the sight
of the hale
and hearty,

those eternal soul-mates,
joined at the lip
never tired
displaying themselves.

It's depressing
to see
a single phoenix
in brocade,

but a pair of lovebirds
glued to the screen
will cheer you up
in no time!

•

The paired lovebirds
glide and flit
around the decorated
beams,

through the turquoise
hangings,
fumes
of turmeric.

Fashionably permed
and teased,
her hair
is cutting-edge.

Eyebrows
pencilled crescents,
next she applies
her war-paint.

•

War-painted
and powdered up,
she exits
to the chase.

Quite
independent
yet appealingly
vulnerable,

she changes
expression more
than is strictly
necessary.

Boys ride by
on thoroughbreds
as dark as
iron cash.

Hookers do trade;
hair in the dragon style,
with bent-knee
golden pins.

•

At City Hall already
birds
are coming home
to roost;

in the gate
of the Supreme Court
sparrows
brawl.

High and mighty
vermilion walls
overlook
the boulevards of jade;

the azure cars
slip down
beyond the golden
barricades.

Joy-riders
on the look-out
roam
the blank estates,

while hit-men
make
their contracts
in full light

and fat cats
in hand-
tooled footware
deal strict cash,

till all are drawn
down the same side-street
to the hookers'
sweet emporium.

•

The hookers
in the darkening
put on
flash stuff,

and then with purest voices
sing
familiar
sentimental airs;

in the outskirts
night on night
figures visit
like the moon,

at the heart
each morning
traffic gathers
like clouds.

•

Both the outskirts
and the city's heart
are conveniently situated
just off the freeway,

while major transportation routes
provide immediate access
to the financial
district.

Supple willows
and green ash
bend
touching the earth,

through sultry air
the red dust
joins
the sinking sky.

•

Now you arrive,
you civil guards
of this our state,
a thousand strong,

to drink
green wine
from nacre
cups.

Gauze boleros,
jewelled zones
are stripped
for you,

for you,
dance turns exotic,
and the throat
grows deep.

•

Then there are the big men
go by the name of
"Minister"
or "General":

the sun and sky
revolve
around them
and they yield to none.

Presuming respect,
these proud spirits
suffer
no reproach,

such high grasping
can't endure
nor recognize
restraint.

•

These great men
unrestrained:
their vehicle
the storm.

They claim
their music
and their sports will last
a thousand years,

offering
their power
and wealth
for our example.

•

In the cycle
of the seasons
change comes
instantaneous,

or
chard
ocean
switch,

gold steps
and white jade halls
become
green pine.

•

Silent
in the emptiness
he dwells,
attentive.

Nothing
is happening
but flowers
on the mountain:

falling always
falling through
his reach
they fall.

a slept
by the stream

woke
beside ice

wisdom
is sudden

nonsense
said b

all gain
is gradual

who would build
a gate of gold
must knock nail
every day

c dropped
a diamond
in water

clothing is luxury
let our heroes adorn it

gone!

truth is a privilege
let our heroes enjoy it

gone!

hope is a gift
let our heroes endure it

gone!

words are too much
let our heroes

are certain
mansions
unguarded?

will every
order
be honoured?

if so then
vouchsafe
intangible
bulk goods

is it that
life is cheap?

if so then
grant
incorrigible
dust

remembrance
forbearance
abstinence
eminence

forgetfulness

a better
place

night driving
dangerous
country roads

the radio
his company

one station
fluctuated

the music
touched him

struggling
to tune
true to that
signal

his headlights

blazed
vertically
into the sky

through the
settling
branches

scattering
birdcalls

slight
bagatelles

snatching
isolated
details
from the
crowd

the way
a mirror
after use
captures
momentarily
a furtive
glance
secret
exchange
covert
solicitation
as it is
slipped
away

darting
brightness
a small
image
of the
day

playing
with a toy
fuck

the city
travelling
upriver

preparing
to dream

determined
to remember
nothing

not past
not future

asleep
in a street
called
you have
forgotten

she has
become
an ancestor

white
vermin
laughs

try the
close-grained
handle
of this
claw-hammer

nestles
in your grip
like a kitten

but without
anxiety

your arms
will be pleased

combine
with our oval
section
wire nails

drive them
deep into
the running
water

Time Up

Weakness blossomed in her extremities, first presenting in her hands and arms an aftermath. She saw herself lose all power over the limbs. On her back perfectly helpless, she seems a skeleton. She saw herself. The strangeness. Every muscle in the body is wasted. Those of the back share in the general atrophy, which, however, is perhaps most florid in the muscles of the hands and arms. Though every muscle in the body is wasted. The fingers are flexed in the characteristic griffin's-claw gesture, the flexion being not of the metacarpo-phalangeal joints but of the phalangeal. The while the hand commands, the interossei seem to have entirely disappeared, so that the finger and thumb of an observer can be made to meet between the metacarpal bones. If the observer pleases? Thank you. The long bones of the arm can be watched throughout their entire length as distinctly as though covered only by integument. The legs and feet are in a very similar condition. They, also, can be watched. So wasted are the abdominal muscles that the spine can be distinctly felt throughout the lumbar region. Too long now you've finished.

Standing Still Requires Awareness

Feeling sadness and joy, they experience even a strange tranquillity. Though there be moral aberration in the governance of the state, a closed man may stay dispassionate.

They report sadness or frustration at their mechanical imprisonment, but none of that terror one would expect. Do they forget those indifferent, nonconscious worlds that whirl with blinding speed in elliptical orbits about a middle-sized yellow-hot star held fast by impersonal mathematical dictates?

No acute fear is evidenced, though the Grand White, or Executioner's Star, portend her velvet plots and cutting edges. Yes! At this, tears may be produced, although the motor accompaniments are missing. Increase the pressure, augment stimulus, still is no further response; introduce the multiple infinities of numbers, of worlds, and find them wasted, provoking neither exaltation nor dread.

The body is no theatre for them, and they can have no dialogue with auspices. When it traverses the War Axe, White foretells the clash of weapons; when it enters the Ghost, it is time to execute vassals. Curiously, the suffering that usually follows pain seems in them to be blunted.

It is impossible to write of such, and not be moved to pity.

terrible
limitation
this

to be forced
to deal only
with what is

out of absence
and ellipsis
to construct
the field
of possibilities

abraded
handles
furrowed
corridors
present
the past
and its futures

an empty chair

because i
was ill
i didn't
come

because
i fell
i can't
walk

this morning
it rained
it will rain
yesterday
was fine
mud is
everywhere

sun
moon
stars

i will go
out into
the sun

hollowing
out the
darkness

nesting
there

sheeted in
with glass
wood lead

and with gold
or silver
skins

bookbinders
endpapers

or fabric
for matting

are still lifes
memories
gardens

listen

uncertain
steps return
always at
night

in the fullness
of the bed
are two troughs

one so shallow
as scarcely
to be
evident

limp
jackets
shirts
hang from a horizontal
spade-handle

suspended
by two
lengths
of blue
plastic rope

there are
shoes

the air
breaks
off

the intent
participants
all stuck
dumbstruck
sans ensemble

each must
identify
its own
particular
attunement

sing
against
silence

a single
tree
cries out
in the storm
even with
the whole
grove
gone

one
smiles
briefly

peels
the smile
tosses it
to another
who must
catch
wear it
then peel
and throw

who smiles
mistakenly
is dead

last
alive
wins

the dead
titter
making
it harder
to stay
alive

bind ankles
with linen

pull on
gloves
of supple
leather

wooden
laths support
the long
limb bones

torso
is wrapped
in tough
synthetics

metals
shield
skull

glass
eyes

script
memory

these are
athletes
preparing
to dream

irregular
whirling
plucks
at everything
drags
it in

surprisingly
even
a sensible
girl and a
solid
fellow
fall so

a quick
dynamic
feeds on
delicate
hesitations
soft
exchanges

this tum
bling bliss
say who can
stand it

the sheets
of wheat
are rolled
back

gone
that blonde
hay
your pillow

uncertain stuff
unseemly judged

all goods
exacted
for the pure
and hostile
fronts

time's shoulder
give you
comfort
when this day
is done

Grief in the king-fort?
With Niall gone, small wonder;
all was fast against affliction,
grievous now.

And will grieve on
abandoned by civility,
though a dynasty outlasted
loneliness from there.

All kings but one
in time relinquish rule.
Who'd want the world?
Grief in the king-fort,
                    grief.

Laughter across the way marks out
the marriage-house;
such loud excess
intrudes a desolation here.

Though happily that bride
may get what she contracted for
some are short-changed
as I hereby lay charge.

You, ruler of the lasting world,
I now denounce,
for killing of my kind, my gentle
loving and most innocent king.

As hostage he'd be worth
thoroughbred herds, goldhoards;
who brought him here would learn
my further kindnesses.

Proper to ransom such a man
could to me show him so kind
delivering me from a one-day's raid
some twelve score head of beef.

Delicate linens, ah! you break
my heart, you, where Niall could sleep sound,
and you, white one, little bed,
you miss him too.

How then should I bear myself
happening upon a shirt
when he it dressed
lies dead in Kells?

Travelling westward from Armagh
Niall put me this:
whichever goes in front,
my love, where should we head?

Straight answer, this, my king,
together in the cool clay
of Ailech, let them lay us
in a single grave.

If you, my love, go first,
in front of me into the earth,
I'll take myself no other queen
but long grieving without
                              laughter.

Kells, occasion for blindness,
since I lay with your king;
Kells, grown disfigured
now Niall is gone.

The first kings I wived,
I augmented their glory,
but Niall was far dearer than both;
Kells, occasion for blindness.

My bright Niall ceased,
my man and my king ceased,
here his broad lands continue;
Kells, occasion for blindness.

Well I remember generous Niall
here on this hill
laughing his wealth away;
Kells, occasion for blindness.

I will walk to the grave of Niall;
there is room where he lies
for me to lie next him;
Kells, occasion for blindness,
                        blindness.

Breaks the heart keening
as the edge keen the king,
keen Niall Blackknee
gracious as great.

[This is doubtful]

Ask what breaks my heart:
keening Niall the bright laughing;
till doomsday the heart hurt
atrociously wasting.

First I came into Munster:
high-king's consort queen
to arch-bishop Cormac
the perfectly-bright.

Then next into Leinster
in which rich realm
though some muttered
I did not starve.

[This transition is difficult]

. . . came Tara's heir,
that true prince,
successor to arch-kings.

Together we shared
childhood in Tara,
concentric city
of the true promised land.

That destroyer of pastures,
that master of plunder,
that fiercest of men,
deepest red amongst Irish.

The place where he fell
broke my heart
[this line is lost]
nor does Donal survive him.

Niall, king, son of kings,
Donal, soft face unfurrowed,
dead detach me from kin,
reduce heart to sheer blood.

I am Gormlaith, the keening:
first husband-king Cormac,
son Donal, fierce Niall,
these three broke my heart.

O King of the stars,
grant mercy to Niall,
O Mary, great queen,
shield this cold keening
                          breaks.

Empty, a fort
stands forewarning to others;
such desolation in a palace
just one trick among life's many.

I miss the princes
hospitable and brave
and grieve
through so much emptiness.

Soon the rest
will make joint desolation;
is this not sign enough?
an empty fort;
           empty.

Rag, patched on patch,
why would I blame you?
not one courtly hand
added craft to your stitch.

In Tara once
alongside Niall of Emain,
happily he honoured me:
I drank from his own cup.

In Limerick once
with loving Niall of Ailech,
my clothes spectacular
among the western chieftains.

When his people gathered
to test their foals for speed
I drank as they drank, wine
from fine horn cups.

Seven score women attended us
in these assemblies
as the race was settled
on the green course of my king.

I am a woman of Leinster,
I am a woman of Meath;
ask which land most dear to me:
no zone of those, but my true king's north.

Brambles snare me,
snarl my rags;
thorn no ally,
briar attacks,
                    rag.

Mourning Niall I survive;
what pain could exceed this?
surplus such days,
me so disfigured.

Bone-weary tonight, I,
all love-words exhausted;
draped Tara quenched too,
all glamour gone out.

Emain silent and dark
where they played once,
hosts gathered
departed.

Utter silence in Oileach:
no music;
Lough Foyle's speech is hoarse;
disfigured, I die.

To the west to the east
each kingdom enfeebled,
it grieves me
their grief.

Sad this north too
my voice strange to its soldiery;
the south dwindles away,
grief blurs my face.

My king, son of kings,
who gave away gold,
dead, stuns the woods;
grief endures.

King Niall Blackknee, his queen,
master of armies, his consort,
now has gossip for counsel;
do you question my
mourning?

Ah! grief my own,
Ah! lost my own love,
destroyed in the night
that king's son went down.

Ah! queen's son set below,
Ah! then what future after,
as giving as brave falls
and the field falls waste after?

Ah! true king now dead
that alive was not halt;
this soul fallen in war,
I chant pity and pain
                              Ah!

Here the hound is neglected
till proven,
the unloved
easily slighted.

The crow's black, say I say,
then, white, they say back;
I go wrong, the same say,
whether striding or bowed.

Bleak the hill without trees,
chill the shoulder unfriended,
and empty the weave without issue,
here, don't I know it?

As she finds in love
from one man satisfaction,
no he ever found
but one woman could please.

That king, son of kings, was my pleasure,
most loved and most brave, that most gentle man
stood head against head
with this child of the arch-king.

I a long age since
in this fort of crude strength,
my force fragile, this frail I,
can't abide
　　　here.

Soft with that foot, Monk,
you stand by a king's side
shovelling covers
on limbs I lay next to.

An age in that dark, Monk,
you've gravelled him down;
an age in his night
he shrinks from the boards.

That son of free giving
earned better than crosses;
sheet him over with stone
but soft with that foot, Monk.

The queen that chants this,
gentle daughter of kings,
craves that stone for her bed-sheet
so soft with that foot, Monk,
                              soft.

Pity the earth constrains you, Niall,
pity us visit your grave!
status and grace stand annulled
now north holds the north's king dead.

A while with the meek,
a while with the mighty;
better than these my while with Niall
who laughed as he drank.

I had banquets with wine,
I had wealth and society;
now Niall walks with saints
what could prevent him Heaven?

Bright but for black knee
Niall had no equal;
such beauty!
the curl, the grey eye.

Now the surge breaks cold,
the wind storms from the west,
generosity sinks to her knees,
the ship shudders.

Fair switches with foul,
harsh wind knows no ceasing,
bud is blasted on branch
just by this death.

Where was joy sits decay;
hard threnody this:
my friend in his blood,
Tara ruined till the world's end,
                          the pity!

Sighing heavy tonight, God!
heaviest yet;
for loss of the son of my own bright Niall
alive I'd walk under the earth.

All friends dwindle and fade
now that Niall is dimmed
the listening ear
hears no laughter.

Note these dead:
father mother and brothers,
and fosterkin, loved and revered,
dead and buried and gone.

Fair one held me high
over vatfuls of gold,
fed me nothing but honey,
count that fair one dead too.

Account also the young
who smiled on my knee
while I gave them a love
as if blood of my blood.

So many have gone
from the yellow-topped earth
yet this grieves me most:
Donal's cheek stroked with clay.

Though weakness and war
hunt the living
this value survives:
the love of the child of your blood.

Sorrow on her
trusts her son
to the care
of the foolish.

Grief on her
sent her son
into chaos
of waters and men.

Donal, son of bright Niall,
and of twelve generations of kings,
those lovers of verse
now past moving.

The child of such ancestry
darkens the sky;
white his hand, white his foot,
my heart heavy
            sighing.

Preach, priest!
with quick benediction
on the great soul
of him, the well-born.

Scholars and clerks
had regard in his reign;
hearsay truly reported
his charity.

Not my boast but Niall's will:
that three hundred horse,
with ten hundred cows
I gave in one day.

Generality dealt with,
his sage sought my gift:
cattle, three hundred head,
cloth, a rich crimson bolt.

I paid off his poets
enough and excess;
may what they then received
serve now his soul.

Sorrow afflict him who sundered us
while yet I lived,
sorrow on him seized my horseman
left me alone.

Sorrow on him struck asunder
my dear friend and myself
would have been in his debt
had he left us as one.

Mark, priest, this my poem,
since a while we are private;
let ear hold what it catch,
then rise, priest, and
preach!

Say, three times thirty,
nine times nine, I've loved,
yet if I now loved twenty more
still it wouldn't satisfy.

For Niall I left
all other loves,
desiring his desire;
who might detain me then?

Among assembled warriors
all trophies fell to him;
yet, encountering such straits,
better I'd loved some serf.

Elaborate cloaks, golden rings,
and strings of thoroughbreds;
broad flood run down to drought,
his goods all gone.

Between heaven and earth,
a white dress and a black cloak
now my sole provisioning;
in Kells of the hundred kings, I starve.

North of the church on Sabbath day
instructed by the gentle touch
of the left hand of my king
I, to the abbot's wife, gave goods.

An orb with golden ornament,
fat cows, two score,
a blue Norse hood, a case of horn,
and thirty ounce of gold.

And she, who has them yet,
repaid me them tonight:
two measures of hard oats,
two eggs from her vast clutch.

By him who lit the sun's fire,
if my Niall of the Black Knee lived,
then, you, you minor abbot's twist,
I'd need no eggs from you!

A roan horse,
a cup, and other articles of gold,
I gave her once, and was returned
a cap, a comb, some sundry pretty cloth.

Wretched be the falsely proud,
wretched they who hoard;
before misfortune struck
remember, poets took my gold.

Who would trade horses
for good verse, may God reward;
if I speak well of Niall, think
what could a poet say, for pay!
                        what say?

Wretched to me
my own homeland,
I'd sooner stay in Ulster
conversing with kings.

Through seventeen years
among this aristocracy
they have dealt with me kindly,
rather kinsfolk than strangers.

I and the mountain lark,
of a muchness our nature:
with the wood within reach
she sleeps in the peat-bog.

Getting so much from Niall
what reason to leave him?
that gentle slender-handed man,
unequalled.

[This development is obscure.]

. . . .
                 wretched.

Niall! pray heaven on his soul!
let every priest pray too;
he knew life's worth,
and my heart, lacking him, grows sick.

That wise head the land obeyed
can't cancel now my grief:
such the incalculable loss;
his speech to me was soft.

His speech to me was sweet:
such the incalculable loss;
I have no taste for words
but beating fists unceasingly.

Beating fists unceasingly,
his death my extreme loss;
and though in triumph he went out,
bitter our affliction now.

Bitter our affliction now
the very churches weep for him;
myself can't limit grief
though enemies deride.

Though enemies deride,
though solidarity lend strength,
with Niall laid low
how now live on?

How now live on
lacking passion, joy and song?
Him who withheld no wealth for self
to mourn demeans each woman well.

Niall! pray heaven on his soul!
to survive him is protracted pain,
that stranger to our company
till judgement day:
                    Niall!

Lamentation has its season
and right end, even for gentle Niall;
excess has delivered me
to this not life not death.

A time of one and thirty years,
since that king died,
each night I wept him
seven hundred tears.

Last night he, my dead king, came in,
said: put an end to mourning, love,
the Arch-King of the seraphim
grows weary hearing you.

I turned on Niall,
angry as I had never been before,
said: for what cause should that highest King
turn weary from a penitent?

Remember, love, he said,
God set all men in being;
why then would he wish
to overhear them weeping?

Then Niall himself
turned from me, twisting love;
at sight of this I scream aloud,
spring after him.

For some support
I leaned my breast
against a bed-post of smooth yew
which penetrated it, my heart.

Tonight I implore God
grant me surcease in death;
on what road Niall turns
let me turn too.

King husband first
three hundred cows,
two hundred horse
conveyed me.

Then my second husband king,
never to seem outdone
in generosity of soul,
conveyed me double that.

Why should I hide
from my true king, these gifts?
Such gifts, and twice such more,
Niall gave me in one month.
                    Lamentation

Notes

Originals of the "Folk Songs from the Finno-Ugric and Turkic Languages," along with rudimentary literal translations, may be found in the Hungaroton set, *Folk Music of Finno-Ugrian and Turkic Peoples*. Similarly, the "Folk Songs from the Hungarian" are worked from the multi-volume *Anthology of Hungarian Folk Music, Hungarian Folk Music of Bukovinian Székelys,* and *Hungarian Folk Music Collected by Béla Bartok, Phonograph Cylinders,* all from Hungaroton.

"To Lily Bloom" was commissioned for *A-N-N-A!* (Lüneburg: zu Klampen, 2000). "Limitless" was commissioned for the colloquium *Roots and Wings: The Poetry of Antón Avilés de Taramancos* (U.C.C., 2003). In both cases originals and literal translations were provided.

The Irish text of the seventeenth-century folk song "Séan O'Duibhir a' Ghleanna" is available, along with a very free version in English by Thomas Furlong, in *Irish Minstrelsy or Bardic Remains of Ireland* by James Hardiman (repr. Shannon: I.U.P., 1971). Originals of both of the "Anonymous Love Songs from the Irish" are given in *Dánta Grádha: An Anthology of Irish Love Poetry, 1350–1750,* collected and edited by Thomas F. O'Rahilly (repr. Cork: Cork U.P., 1976). The second also occurs, with translation, in *Love Songs of Connacht* by Douglas Hyde (repr. Shannon: I.U.P., 1968).

"Outcry" is a working of some of the surviving poems by Juan Chi (pinyin Ruan Ji, 210–263). The standard scholarly account of these in English is *Poetry and Politics* by Donald Holzman (Cambridge: C.U.P., 1976). John Cayley's Wellsweep Press also issued a volume of literary translations of this work, *Songs of My Heart* by Graham Hartill and Wu Fusheng (London: Wellsweep, 1988), and versions of individual poems may be found in many anthologies.

"Capital Accounts" is worked from *Ch'ang-an: Ku-i* by Lu Chao-lin (pinyin Lu Zhaolin, 635–84). Scholarly translations along with notes, commentary and the original Chinese text may be found in both *Flowering Plum and the Palace Lady: Interpretations of Chinese Poetry* by Hans H. Frankel (New Haven: Yale, 1976) and *The Poetry of the Early T'ang* by Stephen Owen (New Haven: Yale, 1977).

The "Love Songs from a Dead Tongue" are worked from Irish originals, some dating back at least to the fifteenth century and perhaps several centuries earlier. They speak in the voice of the famous queen Gormlaith (d. 948 AD), whose three husbands were all kings, the last being Niall Blackknee who, in 919, died in battle with the Norse. Eleven of the originals are presented with scholarly translation by Osborn Bergin in his *Irish Bardic Poetry* (Dublin: Dublin Institute for Advanced Studies, 1970). An additional six have been drawn from the paper "Triamhuin Ghormlaithe" by Anne O'Sullivan, published in *Ériu*, vol. XVI (Dublin, 1952). "Love Songs from a Dead Tongue" is simultaneously published in my *Courts of Air and Earth* (Exeter: Shearsman, 2007), and so far as I am aware this extended sequence of the Gormlaith poems has not previously been published together either in the original or in translation. I would like to express my thanks to Máire Herbert for her advice and encouragement.

The many thirty-six-word poems scattered throughout this volume spring from an attempt to write a large work under rigorous constraints. As the intended structure was conceived as a three-dimensional sestina (the standard form being interpreted as in two dimensions), and since all the structural elements would have been concealed, some of these pieces were published as "From a Phantom Hyper-Sestina." When I realized that the centrifugal forces had overpowered my original intentions for overall coherence, I published some more under the title "Ana" (as in Shakespeareana, Joyceana, etc.). Here I've allowed the principle of dispersal to overcome completely my initial nostalgia for order.

The sequence "Undone" represents another experiment at composition under constraint. A commentary on the structures underlying "The Peacock's Tale" is online at *Drunken Boat* (drunkenboat.com) in the OuLiPo feature of issue #8, and the comments there apply in principle to the other pieces in the sequence.

Much of the contents not already accounted for in these notes comprised my contributions to the online collaborative composition *OffSets* (soundeye.org/offsets/) and some minor alterations have been made to hide the signs of amputation.

Acknowledgements

Some of the pieces included here have been published in the journals/webzines *Shearsman, Masthead, Free Verse, Default, The Long View, Poetry Ireland Review,* and *Wrong;* several also appeared in the chapbooks *Take Over* and *Undone, Say* (The Gig, 2003). "The Peacock's Tale" was included, with a commentary, in *Art, Possibility & Democracy* (Frankfurt: Revolver, 2006) and online at drunkenboat.com.

"STILLSMAN" was included in the Vinyl Project, curated by Simon Cutts (Cork, 2005), and also performed by Art/not Art at EV+a (Limerick, 2006). I wish to thank all the editors and curators responsible.

As always, many and various personal debts are signalled in the dedications to these poems. They represent a network of dependencies without which this book wouldn't have happened. Most particularly, I want to thank both Paula and George for persistent, pertinent, and sometimes unexpected help.

Thanks are also due to the Fulbright Foundation, the Ballinglen Arts Foundation, the Arts Council of Ireland/ An Chomhairle Ealaíon, and Aosdána for important material support.

Contents (expanded view)

316

Folk Songs from the Hungarian